# HEARTS *of* AMISH COUNTRY

# LOVE *Comes* QUIETLY

## Jo Ann Brown

AnniesFiction.com

*Love Comes Quietly*
Copyright © 2017, 2020 Annie's.

All rights reserved. No part of this publication may be reproduced, stored in a retrieval system, or transmitted in any form or by any means—electronic, mechanical, photocopying, recording or otherwise—without the prior written permission of the publisher. The only exception is brief quotations in printed reviews. For information address Annie's, 306 East Parr Road, Berne, Indiana 46711-1138.

The characters and events in this book are fictional, and any resemblance to actual persons or events is coincidental.

Library of Congress-in-Publication Data
*Love Comes Quietly*/ by Jo Ann Brown
p. cm.
I. Title
2017948330

AnniesFiction.com
(800) 282-6643
Hearts of Amish Country™
Series Creator: Shari Lohner
Series Editor: Janice Tate

10 11 12 13 14 | Printed in China | 9 8 7 6 5 4 3 2

# 1

With every step, it became clearer to Leah Kauffman that suitcases on wheels hadn't been designed for an Indiana dirt road. Sure, they'd worked fine during her trip west from Pennsylvania on the train and on two different buses, but their efficiency had vanished as she walked toward her *Grossmammi*'s farm.

Or rather, she *tried* to walk along the road between two fields of corn with drying tassels that reached far above her head. Her pace was the same pattern over and over. Move a half step forward. Stop. Tug. Another half step forward, and repeat. Each stone, no matter its size, seemed eager to catch a wheel and tilt a suitcase in one direction or the other.

She paused and glared at the offending luggage. As she looked over her shoulder, the other suitcase moved and got stuck in the soft dirt, mired more deeply than the first.

"Will you behave?" she asked. When she realized she was talking to her suitcases as if she expected a response, she laughed.

Laughing felt good. She wondered when she'd last laughed. Certainly not since the dreary letter had arrived at her family's farm in Lancaster County, Pennsylvania, last week. It had been from her beloved Grossmammi Ruth, who had moved to Indiana almost five years ago along with Leah's *Grossdawdi*. Grossmammi had been left alone after Grossdawdi Ben had passed away in his sleep three years ago. The whole family in Lancaster County had expected Ruth to return to live in the *Dawdi Haus* attached to the house where she'd raised six *Kinder* as well as having her *Kinskinder* there most days, but Ruth had decided to remain on the small farm that had become her home.

Until she'd read the letter, Leah had imagined Grossmammi the last time she'd seen her. Ruth had come to Lancaster County for a short visit when Leah's older brother, Fred, had married the girl he'd been sweet on since they'd attended school together. Ruth had swept into the house, shooed Leah's widowed *Daed* from the kitchen, ordered Leah to help her, and had taken over preparing meals for the other guests who'd arrived the day of the wedding. Leah had watched in awe as Ruth managed the kitchen with brisk efficiency.

For the next four days, they'd cooked and cleaned, and then cooked and cleaned some more. The wedding had been held at the bride's family's house, but relatives on the Kauffman side had returned to the family farm after the celebrations were over. Leah had spent time with cousins she hadn't seen in months and met the new *Bopplin* who'd been added to the family since her sister Elsie's wedding the year before.

Grossmammi had been a whirlwind, showing no signs of her age and not allowing anyone else to slack off. That was how Leah remembered the older woman she adored.

Until Grossmammi's most recent letter had arrived.

Leah could see the words in the precise handwriting as if they'd been seared into her eyes:

> *This summer has presented more challenges than I expected. By the grace of Gott, I find the strength to rise from my bed each day. The cold I endured last winter stayed far longer than I'd expected. It went on and on despite me dosing myself with echinacea tea and chewing on several cloves of garlic every day until my symptoms eased. Though it's the last week of August, I don't look forward to the chill of winter.*

The hint Ruth might be failing had been enough for Leah to persuade her worried Daed to allow her to travel west to the Indiana districts settled by the Lancaster County Amish. She'd hesitated for a moment, wondering if he'd be okay on his own. However, her sister Elsie lived next door, and she would make sure Daed had food on his table and clean shirts.

It wasn't as if Leah expected to be gone forever. Once she discovered what was amiss with Grossmammi, she'd find the right combination of herbs and foods to get her on track. Leah couldn't imagine anything keeping the older woman down for long. Not even the death of Grossdawdi Ben had slowed Ruth Kauffman—she'd continued to work on the Indiana farm as if she were a young bride.

Leah hoped she'd brought the right herbs with her. From the time Leah could walk and understand simple words, Ruth had taught her about healing herbs. She had studied more on her own in the five years since her grandparents had left Pennsylvania, and she'd brought a variety in her smaller suitcase. Maybe one would strengthen her Grossmammi and help her regain her vigor.

With another jerk Leah yanked both suitcases along the road. She moved closer to the middle of the road where there were fewer stones. When the wheels rolled more easily, she smiled. She increased her pace, eager to see Grossmammi.

A rapid motion caught her eye. Something rushed between two rows of corn. Like a bull released from a field, a small shape slammed into her.

Leah fought for balance. Small arms encircled her waist the moment before she lost the battle to stay on her feet. The suitcases' handles clattered against the stones. She realized just before hitting the dirt road that she'd been struck by a Kind.

She wrapped her arms around the little one, twisting to make sure she didn't fall on top of the Kind. A wave of pain washed over her as her right knee hit a stone, and a cry burst from her lips. She'd protected the little . . . girl, she realized when she saw the Kind lying on the ground beside her.

Black shoulder-length hair hid most of the little girl's face, but Leah guessed by her size that she must be around four or five years old. She wore denim jeans with garish green and pink patches on the knees and a bright blue T-shirt with a cartoon character on the front.

She wasn't an Amish Kind—that much was clear by her clothing.

"Are you okay?" Leah asked, wincing as she moved her right leg. Her knee felt as if someone had struck it with a hammer. Tears welled in her eyes, but she ignored them as she bent toward the little girl whose feet were tangled with Leah's legs. The Kind was crying silently, large tears cascading along her cheeks.

"Are you okay?" Leah asked again.

The little girl clung to her and sobbed without making a sound.

Looking around, Leah couldn't help wondering. What was the Kind running from?

James Holden stopped midstep as he pushed past the last sharp leaves on the cornstalks. His daughter, Abby, was in a pile on the road with a dark-haired woman. An *Amish* woman, he realized when the woman brushed the dirt off her simple cranberry cape dress and adjusted her heart-shaped organdy head covering—as well as she could with Abby apparently glued to her, anyway. Her fingers lingered against her skull. Had it collided with the ground? When she grimaced as she touched her knee, he wanted to groan aloud.

This could make his work on Amish property uncomfortable or impossible. He guessed the plain folk would forgive a child, but they might not be willing to overlook a father who couldn't control his five-year-old daughter. Every Amish child he'd seen—no matter how young—seemed well-behaved. At first, he'd thought it was because the kids were on their best behavior in the presence of an *Englischer*, as they called outsiders. In the past couple of weeks, though, he'd observed the children playing and doing chores when they weren't aware of him. They'd been just as calm.

More calm than Abby ever had been.

On the other hand, they hadn't watched their mother die in a car accident.

Pushing out of the cornfield, he rushed to help the Amish woman to her feet and gently disentangled her from his daughter. He spotted two black suitcases and quickly squashed his curiosity about why she'd been pulling them along the uneven road.

Once he was sure the woman was stable on her feet, James knelt beside his daughter. Sweet Abby didn't usually take off like a rabbit with a dog chasing it, but she'd been frightened by a swarm of bees near a tree he'd been studying. She'd almost disappeared from sight by the time he'd realized she'd fled. His longer paces had closed the distance between them, but he hadn't caught her before she'd barreled into the Amish woman.

He ran his hands over his daughter's legs and arms, and reassured himself no bones had been broken. He didn't see a single scratch on her, though there was a red spot on her elbow which might become a bruise. Aware of the woman looking at him, he lifted Abby into his arms and hugged her.

His daughter hid her face against his shoulder. James wasn't sure if she was hurt or scared or ashamed. It could have been any of those.

He hadn't done a good job of guessing what his daughter thought since Connie's death a year ago.

The familiar pang squeezed his heart as it did every time he thought about his wife. He refused to believe that her death had been anything other than a horrible accident. The rumors he'd heard whispered couldn't be true. He'd reminded himself over and over that it wasn't easy for anyone to accept that a person halfway through her twenties had died abruptly.

Knowing he needed to apologize on Abby's behalf, James raised his eyes toward the plain woman. *Nobody should use the word "plain" when describing her*, he thought. Her clothing might be plain, but she was beautiful.

Her dark hair was pulled back at her nape and hidden under a white head covering. Sunlight burnished the ebony strands with blue highlights. Her eyes were as warm and liquid as maple syrup and a few shades darker. He wondered if, when she smiled, the expression on her apple-cheeked face would be as sweet.

James realized he was gaping at her like a boy who'd discovered girls were no longer an annoyance. Knowing he needed to say something, he asked, "Are you all right?"

"I'm fine." She brushed her black apron, but the dirt stuck.

"I'm sorry Abby ran into you."

"It was an accident." Checking to make sure her head covering was in place, she reached toward her suitcases.

"Let me." He put Abby down and grabbed the handle of the closest bag at the same time she did.

When their fingers touched, he was astounded by the spark that arced from her skin to his.

*Static electricity*, he told himself, though he knew how unlikely that was. *It couldn't be anything else.* The thought was almost a scold.

When it came to dating, the Amish focused on people among their own.

Dating? Now where had *that* thought come from? He hadn't thought about dating since Connie's death. He wasn't ready to risk his splintered heart again, even if he had the time, which he didn't. Between being father *and* mother to his daughter, who had miraculously escaped the wrecked car, and his work on preparing his doctoral thesis for his PhD in botany, he barely had time for eating and sleeping. When he could combine parenting and work—as he'd tried to do today by taking Abby with him—he counted himself fortunate.

Lifting the woman's other suitcase, he set it next to the one she was lowering to the road. She squatted as she unzipped the bag.

"Do you need help?" he asked, though he knew if he had any sense he'd tell her goodbye and take Abby home.

"I'm fine," she repeated. She moved her hands through her suitcase. "I'm almost to my Grossmammi's house. My grandmother's house."

"Like Little Red Riding Hood?" The words slipped out before he could halt them.

When she glanced at him and away, he thought he caught the hint of a smile, but he couldn't be sure.

He wouldn't have blamed her if she was furious with him and Abby.

Looking at the little girl who hid her face against his leg, he sighed. His daughter hadn't meant any harm. She'd been frightened by the bees. He didn't have an excuse. That he was unsettled by his unexpected reaction to a pretty Amish woman didn't give him carte blanche to say stupid things.

The woman sat on her heels and sighed with obvious relief. "Everything is undamaged."

"Everything?" he asked before he could stop himself.

When she glanced at him, he started to apologize, but she cut him off with a smile. He'd been right. Her smile was charming and lit her face as if she'd swallowed a bit of sunshine.

"I was checking," she said, "to make sure the herbs I brought for my grandmother were okay. According to her most recent letter, she's not been well."

"I'm sorry." Finally he'd said the right thing.

"*Danki.* I mean, thank you."

He chuckled. "I guessed that. I'm glad everything's okay in your bag."

"I wasn't worried about the dandelion root and ginseng. They're in tight containers. However, the nettle and peppermint leaves spilled on the way here, and I want to be certain there's enough to make Grossmammi a revitalizing tea."

Though his botanical studies didn't include herbs, James had heard enough from his colleagues to know healing with herbs and other alternative medicines wasn't nonsense. He was impressed by this young woman's obvious knowledge of herbal remedies.

The woman zipped her bag shut and stood again. She was tiny, he realized, so short her head would have fit under his chin if he drew her into his arms.

*Enough!* Maybe that was why he was enjoying the idea of getting to know her better. It probably wouldn't be possible given his schedule with teaching and research, so there was no reason not to enjoy their brief conversation. He had to admit he was curious about who she was and why she was tugging two suitcases along the country road. Even so, if he had half a brain, he'd end the encounter now.

He didn't.

"I'm James Holden," he said. "This whirlwind is my daughter, Abby."

At her name, his daughter peered in the woman's direction.

"Hi, Abby," the woman replied. "I hope you're okay too."

His daughter hid her face again, but he noticed she kept sneaking glances at the woman. That surprised him, because Abby had avoided people other than him for the past year.

"I'm Leah." The woman smiled, and he felt a surprising skip in his heartbeat. "Leah Kauffman."

He should have guessed. There were two farms farther along this road: the Eichers' farm and the Kauffmans'. As far as he knew, only an elderly man and two younger men around James's own age lived at the Eicher place, so the Kauffman farm must be Leah's destination. He'd seen an elderly woman working in the garden there.

"Nice to meet you, Leah." He gave her an apologetic smile. "I'm sorry we had to meet under these circumstances." He explained how he and Abby had chanced upon a large swarm of bees in a tree.

"Were you stung?" Leah asked.

Something about the concern in her voice threatened to bring forth emotion he'd kept submerged for the past year. He'd been surrounded by cautious sympathy from those who didn't know how to say they were sorry, but there was nothing lukewarm in Leah's response. She sounded as if she cared—and he believed she truly did.

His reaction to her concern frightened him as much as Abby had been scared by the bees. Because if he began to feel good things, he had to face the bad ones as well. He wasn't ready to do that.

Leah saw a storm of emotions cross the Englischer's face, and she wondered if he found this conversation as odd as she did. Something wasn't quite right, but she couldn't guess what. He was being nice, and the little girl had stopped crying.

Yet something felt amiss.

She tried to be patient as she waited for James to answer. How difficult could it be? He'd either been stung by the swarming bees or he hadn't. Had his daughter been stung? Leah hadn't seen any sign, but bees aroused by anger often crawled under clothing to sting. Either way, she wished James would answer, so that if they'd been stung, she could offer him and the little girl lavender oil to ease the pain. Otherwise she should be on her way.

She was instantly contrite. The *gut* Lord had put a love of herbs into her heart and brought people into her life to help her learn how to use them to ease pain. With His gift came the responsibility to offer succor to any who needed her help. She shouldn't be thinking of hurrying away. *Ja*, she was worried about Grossmammi, but that was no excuse to wish this handsome Englischer would quit hesitating and answer her question.

*He is handsome*, she thought. His hair was darker than hers, as black as a moonless night, but his blue eyes reminded her of the lake where she'd gone boating last summer. With a square jaw emphasized by the shadow of whiskers, his features drew her eyes more than they should.

"I wasn't stung," he finally said.

Lost in her contemplation of his strong profile, she stumbled over her words. "Th–Th–That's *gut*."

James glanced at his daughter. "Were you stung, Abby?"

The little girl shook her head, but wrapped her arms around herself as if to ward off more bees. She leaned against her dad's leg again, and he put his hand on her shoulder. This time she didn't hide her face. Instead she stared at Leah with the candid gaze of a Kind.

"That's *gut*." Leah said again, relieved she didn't stutter this time. She gave the little girl a cautious smile, but Abby's countenance didn't change. She looked as serious as a bishop on a church Sunday.

*Such a strange expression for a little girl!*

"Well, we'd better get going," James said. "We're staying at the Maple Shade Bed and Breakfast in Stony Brook. The owner is a personal friend and she is expecting us for dinner. Being late would be rude." He gave Leah another of his boyish grins. "Before we go, let me say again that I'm sorry Abby ran into you. I hope you can forgive her."

"Of course. Our Lord taught us to forgive one another as He forgives us."

James looked away. Leah wondered if her words had made him uncomfortable. Why? Was it possible he didn't believe in God? If so, she prayed he'd soon find his way to their heavenly Father.

When he didn't reply, the silence felt like an elephant sitting on her shoulders. To ease its weight, she said, "Enjoy your dinner."

"Thank you." He took his daughter by the hand, and Leah watched them walk away.

Only when they had vanished around a bend in the road did she realize what had seemed wrong. During the whole conversation, the little girl hadn't said a word.

Not a single one.

# 2

Leah wanted to cheer when, almost a mile farther along the road, she reached the mailbox with the name *Kauffman* painted on each side in simple white letters. Its flag was shaped like a blue jay. That bird was one of the things Grossmammi had told her to look for.

She took a deep breath. It was time to focus on helping Grossmammi and put handsome James Holden and his silent daughter out of her mind.

Was that possible?

Why hadn't the little girl made a sound, even when she was crying?

*Lord, You know the truth about Abby. Help me see that the fact that You know is enough.*

The short prayer gave her comfort, but it didn't do anything to ease her bafflement.

Leah took a single step and flinched. Her right knee ached from where it'd hit the ground. She guessed when she took off her socks later that night, she'd find a spreading bruise. Grossmammi had kept parsley-filled ice cubes in her freezer when Leah was young. The cubes eased pain and swelling for any bump or bruise. Would Grossmammi have them on hand now there were no Kinder in her house? If not, Leah had brought a packet of ground parsley and would make tea with a couple of teaspoons of parsley and half a cup of water.

The simple solution had been the first herb she'd been taught to use for healing when she'd been close to Abby's age.

*Why was the little girl so shy she couldn't bring herself to say "goodbye"?* Leah wondered.

*Abby's Daed...*

Leah was grateful she was alone. Was she blushing as she thought of James Holden? She'd spoken with many Englischers at auctions and "mud sales," where the plain and Englisch communities mingled. She'd taken on a few students to teach about herbs, and one had been an Englisch man. He'd been close to her Daed's age, but she'd treated him as she did her plain students.

Yet a mere glance from James had disconcerted her. Not in an ill-at-ease way. More in an abrupt awareness of everything he or she did. Every sense seemed to be *more*. She wasn't sure how else to explain it to herself.

Leah shook her head to dislodge the bothersome thoughts. *Why am I thinking about a man I'll never see again? Ja, he was kind and gentle and thoughtful. His apology was genuine, and there can be no doubt how much he cares about his daughter.*

However, *kind* and *gentle* and *thoughtful* were words she could use to describe many people she'd met. They didn't linger in her thoughts as James did.

*Mr. Holden.* That's how she should think of him because he was an Englischer. No, she shouldn't be thinking about him at all!

Leah looked along the farm lane in front of her, needing to focus on something other than *gut*-looking James Holden. At its end was a house that could have been lifted right from the heart of Lancaster County and set among the gentle rolling hills of eastern Indiana. It was white and rambling, a sure sign one wing contained a Dawdi Haus, the small apartment where parents retired when one of their Kinder took over running the farm. For years Leah had assumed that her grandparents would live in the four rooms attached to the family's house in Pennsylvania. Instead they'd decided to move to Wayne County, Indiana.

Early fall flowers were planted on either side of the porch steps. Yellow and orange chrysanthemums bobbed a welcome on slender stems. Beyond the house an expansive garden was visible. She could identify beans and pumpkins and peppers and peas growing in well-groomed rows.

Though the house was familiar, the round barn beyond it wasn't. Only a few round barns existed in Lancaster County, where most farms had bank barns built into a hill. The remaining round barns were now inns or restaurants for the tourists who came for a taste of plain life. She wondered where cows were milked and how rectangular bales of hay were stored in a round hayloft.

A smaller herb garden set between the house and what looked to be a low-slung chicken coop caught Leah's eyes. She hadn't doubted that her grandmother would have plenty of herbs ready to be harvested now that summer was slipping toward autumn. How many hours had Leah spent working alongside her Grossmammi while she discovered the difference between weeds and worthwhile plants? While other Kinder had been busy at the swimming hole or pushing their scooters along the road, she'd plucked tomatoes and beans or pulled onions and carrots. More pleasant times had been spent canning the vegetables and preparing the herbs so they'd be ready when needed.

Grossmammi needed her now.

That thought spurred Leah's feet. She strode forward along the farm lane, ignoring the sharp stabs in her knee, and then came to an abrupt halt.

The gravel lining the farm lane had caught in the wheels on the suitcases. It was going to be even more of a challenge to pull them now. With a grimace, she stepped into the mown grass to the left. Pulling the suitcases remained a struggle, but it was far easier.

Leah was almost to the house when the front door burst open.

The screen door slammed against the wall and an excited voice called, "You're here! You're here at last!"

Ruth was shorter than Leah, but stood as straight as a woman half her age. Years of hard work on the family's farm in Pennsylvania and more in Wayne County had left wrinkles in her sun-browned face. Her hair remained as black as it'd been when Leah was a toddler.

Leaving her bags on the grass, Leah ran to the house. She realized she'd been more worried about the older woman than she'd guessed.

When Grossmammi ran to meet her and drew her into an embrace, Leah was puzzled. Nothing about the older woman suggested she'd slowed down in any way. In fact, she appeared to have far more energy than Leah did after her journey.

Had Leah misunderstood what she'd read in the letter? If she had, her Daed had as well.

"*Ach*, Leah, you're a blessed sight for sore eyes," Ruth said as she appraised Leah from head to toe. "You look *wunderbaar* and as cute as a spring lamb. How was your trip?"

"Grossmammi . . ." Leah wasn't sure where to begin. She didn't want to be blunt and ask why the letter had suggested Grossmammi was in need of help. If it'd been her own mistake, she couldn't take the older woman to task.

"Now you look confused."

"I am. I thought—I mean, I believed—"

"Let's talk about that later. For now, I want you to meet a couple of people you'll be seeing a lot of." She motioned toward two men who were descending the porch steps. "Leah, these fine-looking gentlemen are my neighbors Perry Eicher and his grandson Seth. They live on the farm next door with Seth's brother Willard. And *this*," she said with a bit too much pride for an Amish matriarch, "is my Leah."

Leah would have known the two men were related even if Ruth

hadn't introduced them. Their faces were as round as pumpkins beneath light-brown hair. They had pale-blue eyes the color of winter ice, but there was nothing cold about them as they smiled. Seth was a finger's breadth taller than his grandfather, but they both were dressed in black broadfall trousers and light-green shirts beneath their suspenders. The only real differences—other than their ages and the fact Perry had a beard reaching halfway down his chest—were their boots. Seth's were worn from hours of work, while Perry's looked as if they'd just come out of the box.

Smiling, Leah greeted the two men before giving Ruth another hug.

Ruth asked Seth to collect Leah's bags and bring them into the house. Not giving anyone else a chance to speak, she herded Perry and Leah toward the back door.

When Leah walked inside, it was as if she'd returned in a single step to Pennsylvania. The kitchen's wooden floors and simple cupboards and counter, along with the large table with benches and chairs surrounding it, could have been found on any farm in Lancaster County. The off-white walls were broken up by two windows overlooking the side yard as well as a window above the sink. In addition to the door Leah had come through, two more were located on the wall to the left. The wall in front of her contained a broad doorway leading into the living room, which was large enough to seat the *Leit* on a church Sunday.

The kitchen smelled of freshly baked bread and the spicy tang of whatever was in the oven. Leah felt right at home when she saw the familiar feed-store calendar on the wall along with the short-case clock that had been Grossdawdi's wedding gift to Ruth.

Leah followed Ruth's instructions to sit at the table, giving her a chance to watch and appraise Grossmammi. The older woman scurried about, getting four cups and pouring strong *Kaffi*. She brought them to the table and set them in front of Leah and the Eicher men who had chosen chairs on the opposite side of the table.

"Grossmammi, let me help," Leah said, though she knew the offer was futile.

Once Ruth Kauffman decided to do something—even something as simple as insisting her granddaughter sit while Ruth gathered the makings for coffee and a snack—nobody would get her to change her mind.

As Leah had expected, Ruth *tut-tutted* before saying, "You've come a long way, Leah. Get to know our neighbors. There's plenty of time for you to help later."

"She's bossy," murmured Perry as he gave Leah a wink, "but she's right more than any of the rest of us want to admit."

Leah smiled, liking the elderly man. He'd described Grossmammi perfectly.

She glanced toward Perry's grandson, Seth. He was, she guessed, about a decade older than her own twenty-three years. No hint of a beard was visible, so he must be unmarried. That surprised her, because few Amish men remained unwed into their thirties. Most men wanted to begin a family, so the Kinder would be of an age to help around the farm as soon as possible.

Perry's question about her trip drew her attention back to him. As she spoke with the older man, Seth remained as silent as Abby Holden had been. *Was Seth shy too? Or are there other reasons he doesn't speak?*

A low rumble of a headache warned her that she must have banged her head harder than she'd thought. Though she had to admit, the pain might come from the many questions ricocheting against her skull. A good night's rest would be the best way to banish her headache. If it persisted, she could make tea with valerian to ease the thudding in her head.

When Ruth joined them at the table, she had questions of her own about Leah's journey and the family in Pennsylvania.

Leah answered and passed along the messages she'd been given. There were so many. *I should have written them down to make sure I didn't forget any.*

"Perry," Ruth said, "your cup is empty. I know how much you like my strong Kaffi. Let me get you another cup."

"No." Leah stood. "I'll get it. I sat for a long time on the way here, and it'll be *gut* for me to walk around."

She wasn't surprised that her right knee was a bit stiff as she walked to the gas stove.

She knew she'd failed to hide her pain when Grossmammi asked, "Why are you limping?"

"I got bumped into on the way here." She related what had happened when she met James and Abby Holden, saying nothing about how the little girl hadn't said a single word.

The thought troubled her. A mum Kind was an oddity. None of the Kinder she knew at home could stay quiet long.

"Did you say they were running from a swarm of bees?" Seth asked, speaking for the first time since she'd arrived. His voice was deep.

Leah nodded, but she noticed as she put the refilled cup on the table that Ruth and Perry were frowning at Seth. *Why?*

"Ja," Leah replied. "The little girl was frightened and ran away." Taking her seat again, she tried not to wince as the movement sent a fresh wave of pain through her knee.

"What kind of bees were in the swarm?" Seth seemed to be thinking only about the bees. "Were they honeybees by any chance?"

"I don't know. I didn't see them."

Seth ran his fingers through his hair, paying no attention to the spikes he'd created. Leaning toward her, he asked, "Did they say where the bees were?"

"In a tree, I think."

"Where?"

Ruth interjected, "If you haven't guessed, Leah, Seth is a beekeeper." Ruth eyed her as if eager for Leah's reaction to the statement. "A successful beekeeper. His honey is sold around the county and in Ohio. You should ask him to give you a tour of his hives soon."

Leah bit back a response that she was here to help Grossmammi, not to sightsee. If Grossmammi wanted to pretend in front of her neighbors that she was hale, Leah must keep her concerns to herself for now.

"I'm sure that would be interesting," she replied in a tone she hoped didn't commit her to anything until she discovered what was going on with Grossmammi.

She realized she didn't have to worry because Seth said, as if talking to himself, "If they're honeybees, I can collect them and put them in a hive. After all, the bees will be looking for a new home now that the old one has been disrupted."

"Seth . . ." Perry cautioned in a tone that sounded as if he did so frequently.

Leah wanted to say Seth's questions didn't bother her. It was clear he loved honeybees as she loved herbs. She understood working hard to learn everything you could about a subject. Though neither James nor Seth had mentioned the weight of her larger suitcase, they must have noticed. She'd brought a half dozen books on herbs with her to Indiana—two she always referred to and four more she was looking forward to reading for the first time.

"I think," she said in the silence as Seth and his Grossdawdi exchanged a glance she couldn't decipher, "I'm the wrong person to ask. James Holden and his daughter are the ones who saw the swarm."

"Do you know where they are now?" Seth turned to her, and she saw the candid eagerness in his eyes. He was excited about the bees.

"James mentioned they were staying at a bed-and-breakfast in the village."

"It's got to be the Maple Shade Bed and Breakfast," Ruth said as she passed the sugar bowl to Perry. "It's the only bed-and-breakfast in town."

"Ja, that's the name of the place he mentioned."

"Would you introduce me to him?" Seth looked as shy as Abby again.

"Of course."

"It'll need to be as soon as possible, because the swarm may move in its search for a new home."

Ruth smiled. "Why don't you take him to meet Mr. Holden tomorrow, Leah? If you don't mind, you could do some errands for me in town at the same time." She glanced at the older man as she added, "It'll take care of two things in one fell swoop."

Later, as Leah bid Ruth's neighbors goodbye, she realized she'd never had a chance to agree with the plan. Seth had been so enthusiastic about her Grossmammi's suggestion that he'd answered for both of them.

That wasn't what unsettled her. What bothered her was how much she was looking forward to seeing James and his daughter again. She wanted to get an explanation about why Abby hadn't spoken. That's what she told herself anyway, trying to ignore other reasons for her eagerness to see the Englischers again.

# 3

Leah guessed that if someone had come forward in time from a hundred years ago, the village of Stony Brook would appear pretty much the same to them. The three-story buildings facing each other across a wide street were painted a rainbow of colors. Striped awnings hung over wide shop windows and decorated the upper stories. False fronts rose above the roofs, many of them constructed with the name of the original tenant and the year the building had been built. Brick and wood and what Leah guessed was native stone decorated the ground floors and drew her eyes to the products for sale.

As she walked along the sidewalk, stepping aside for strollers and nodding to those she passed, Leah discovered that the shops sold everything from shoes to computers. Two diners as well as a bakery emitted scents that made her mouth water, though she'd eaten a big breakfast.

She tried not to think about why Grossmammi had avoided any discussion about her letter. Last night Grossmammi had insisted Leah must be too tired. Leah tried to introduce the subject again during breakfast, but had been interrupted by Perry Eicher's arrival.

Seth hadn't been feeling well when he woke. Leah had offered to come to the Eicher farm to deliver herbal relief for Seth's stomach, but Perry insisted the best way to help was locating the swarm.

So Leah had come to the village on her own. Following the directions Ruth had given her before the older woman had left with Perry to tend to his sick grandson, Leah discovered Maple Shade Bed and Breakfast sat behind trimmed hedges and a white picket fence one block off Stony Brook's main street. A small sign by the neat sidewalk leading to the wide porch was the only hint it wasn't a private home.

The navy-blue house was a square block with tall, narrow windows. Wide white shutters stood sentinel on either side of the double doors with etched glass set into them. White rocking chairs invited passersby to stop and sit and chat.

Leah saw a gray buggy, identical to the ones she was familiar with in Pennsylvania, amid the two cars and one garish red pickup in the driveway. A small barn peeking around the right corner of the house was edged by a small pasture where a black horse was grazing. One of the guests, or more likely an employee, must be plain.

Leah climbed the front steps. The porch floor had been painted the same red as the roses growing on the bushes along the picket fence. The porch's ceiling was painted the pale blue of a summer morning sky.

She paused when she reached the varnished front door. Where was the doorbell? Should she knock? While she was accustomed to walking into a plain house without knocking, Englischers had different customs, including doorbells to announce visitors.

Before she could decide what to do, the door opened, and a smiling redhead stepped out. She wore an organdy *Kapp* like Leah's and a cape dress the shade of pine trees in the last light of the day. In one hand she carried a spray can and a dust rag.

"The doorbell is here." The redhead pointed to a knob Leah hadn't noticed in the center of the right-hand door. She pulled on it. When she released the knob, the rattle of a bell could be heard from inside.

"I wouldn't have guessed that was the doorbell if I'd stood here a thousand years," Leah said with a laugh.

"Don't worry. Most people don't. I think Myra keeps it there as a conversation starter for guests." She must have noticed Leah's confusion, because she added, "Myra Andrews owns the Maple Shade Bed and Breakfast." She dimpled. "I'm Dorcas Troyer, the housekeeper, cook, and chief jane-of-all-trades here."

Leah smiled at the exuberant Dorcas. "I'm Leah Kauffman. I arrived yesterday from Lancaster County."

"Oh, you must be Ruth Kauffman's granddaughter. She's been so excited about you coming to visit."

Leah chuckled. "I can see nothing stays secret around here."

"You're right. Have you met your Grossmammi's best friends?"

"Not yet."

"Oh, you've got a treat ahead of you. They're my *Aenti* Naomi Byler and her cousins Vera Jean and Ida Mae Mast. What one of them knows, the other three know. What they all know becomes general knowledge. They're more up to date than the *Stony Brook Daily Independent*, our local newspaper." Dorcas grinned, her blue eyes crinkling. Opening the door again, she said, "*Komm* in."

"Danki."

Leah's eyes grew wide as she entered the bed-and-breakfast. The decor was enthusiastically Victorian. Milled woodwork in a multitude of patterns adorned the walls and hung in the corners of three wide arches opening off the entry foyer. A wide staircase disappeared at a sharp angle to her right. In front of the red flocked wallpaper, lamps hung with thick fringe sat on tables draped in white tablecloths.

It was the complete opposite of a plain house. Every flat surface was covered with bric-a-brac, and the walls in the two rooms on either side of the foyer were painted in bright shades of blue and yellow.

"It takes getting used to," Dorcas said with a smile. "When I started working here, my eyes were tired at the end of the day. Myra says it's authentic and her guests expect it. Me? I try to keep everything dusted."

Leah laughed. "That's a big task."

"You've got no idea. May I ask you a question?"

"Of course."

"I've heard you're an expert herbalist."

"Grossmammi has forgotten more than I know."

Dorcas waved aside her modesty. "Do you focus on cooking or healing herbs?"

"I'm interested in both."

"Will you teach me about cooking herbs?" Dorcas asked. "I think our guests would like foods with more layers of flavors than I've been able to manage. Nobody's said anything, but I can see the disappointed expressions on our guests' faces when I serve orange-bran muffins at breakfast for the second time in three days."

"I'd be glad to teach you."

"*Gut.* I have Wednesdays off as well as Sundays, so maybe you could give me lessons on Wednesdays."

"I'd be delighted." That was the truth. Though she'd just met Dorcas, she had a feeling she and the redhead could become *gut* friends.

James was walking toward the front door of the bed-and-breakfast when he stopped so fast that Abby, who was holding his hand, was almost jerked off her feet. His daughter looked at him in bafflement, something he caught from the corner of his eye, because his gaze was riveted on an amazing sight in the guest lounge.

*What is Leah Kauffman doing at the bed-and-breakfast?*

When his heart did an unexpected flip-flop before racing as if he'd run a marathon, he ignored it and walked into the lounge.

"Leah, I didn't expect to see you here." James clamped his lips together so he didn't say the rest of what he was thinking. He was delighted to have the chance to talk with her again so soon.

The pretty brunette had been ever-present in his mind since their chance meeting yesterday. Somehow her warm smile brightened the lounge with its dark walnut wainscoting and heavy Victorian furniture. A warm glow rushed through each one of his nerves.

He was astonished by his own reaction because he'd been numb for the past year. When Abby pushed past him and went to look up at Leah, he was shocked.

When Leah smiled, Abby remained stone-faced, but James sensed the slightest lessening of her stiff posture. Had Leah somehow reached past the walls Abby had erected, walls he had been unable to breach?

"*Gute Mariye.*" Leah dimpled. "I mean good morning. I'm glad you're here. I wasn't sure how long you would be."

"We're living here for the next few days while our house is fumigated. Termites."

Her nose wrinkled, and he wondered if she had any idea how adorable that expression was. "One of our neighbors in Pennsylvania had termites, and we had to keep a close eye to make sure we didn't get infested too. Our neighbors thought the termites came from a shipment of wood from another part of the state."

"I've got no idea where ours came from, but we'll be glad when they're gone." He put his hands on Abby's shoulders. "Won't we?"

His daughter glanced at him before hurrying over to look out the window facing the street.

James struggled not to sigh in dismay. Looking at Leah, he said, "Oh! I should have asked right away. How's your grandmother?"

"Fine." Her voice was clipped. "It would seem that I read a meaning into her letter she may not have intended."

"Really?"

Her good humor resurrected itself. "Have you met my Grossmammi Ruth, James?"

"I may have. Stony Brook is a small place, and plain folk often come into town."

"If you'd met her, you'd remember her. She speaks her mind."

He smiled in spite of his worry about Abby. "That describes plenty of people in Stony Brook. Few secrets are kept for long in this town."

"So I've heard." She grinned. "Are you busy? I wanted to talk to you."

He understood the cliché about being knocked over by a feather. He was so shocked by her words that the slightest breeze would have sent him off his feet.

"You did?" he asked. "About what?"

"How is she?" Her eyes cut to where Abby was toying with the curtains. "Did the incident with the bees give her nightmares?"

Motioning for Leah to take a seat on the rose-colored settee gave him time to pull his thoughts together. She had surprised him again. He hadn't expected her first question about Abby to be about his daughter's terror. Everyone else he'd met in the past year had been focused on why Abby was mute.

"She had a pretty bad nightmare last night," he said quietly, so his voice wouldn't carry to where Abby had pulled a book off a shelf and was paging through it. "I'm sure it was because of the bees."

"I'm sorry to hear that."

"When we get home, she might put the whole of it behind her." He chose a chair facing where Leah sat with her hands folded on her lap. "We'll be glad to be home. I miss my office."

"What do you do?"

Unsure if she was being polite or delaying the discussion of what had brought her to the bed-and-breakfast, he said, "I teach at Eastern

Indiana Mennonite College while I'm working on my PhD at Miami University in Ohio."

"What do you teach?"

"Botany, but my area of interest focuses on trees."

Her eyes widened. "How they grow and how to keep them healthy?"

"Yes."

"What a wunderbaar thing to teach! Whenever we can help others learn about the gifts God gave to mankind and how to use them and preserve them for the future, we're doing His work." She smiled. "I'm repeating what Grossmammi told me when she taught me about which herbs help us. I'm hoping to learn more from her while I'm here."

"I think my college is offering alternative-medicine courses in the nursing and premed departments." He smiled. "The college was founded by Mennonites, so there's a strong emphasis on majors leading to a lifetime of service, such as teaching or medicine."

"And studying trees?"

"It would take a lifetime to see them all, wouldn't it?" He smiled to cover the pinch of discomfort that reminded him how far he'd strayed from his Mennonite roots.

"You teach at a Mennonite college, but you don't look plain."

He glanced at his blue jeans and simple white shirt, which could have belonged to any plain man. However, instead of suspenders he wore a brown belt.

"My family is liberal, so we resemble what you'd call Englischers."

"We Amish don't have as many variations as the Mennonites do." Leah smiled again. "Though you wouldn't know it by how many different kinds of buggies we drive, or how our Kapps vary, or the width of the brim of a man's hat. We're more alike than we are different, though, when it comes to worshiping God and living a life close to what Jesus taught." A sudden flush climbed her cheeks. He understood why when she added, "I shouldn't be keeping you from whatever you planned to do."

"I was going to drive to the southern part of the county and meet with a man who, I've been told, knows where the beech trees I'm looking for might be." He gave her a grin to put her at ease. "I don't have an appointment with him, so I'm in no hurry to run off."

She sat a bit straighter. "I'm here on behalf of my Grossmammi's neighbor, Seth Eicher. He has beehives, and he was interested when he heard that you saw a swarm. Could you tell if they were honeybees?"

"I think they were honeybees. I know they weren't hornets. If they had been, I would have been running away with Abby rather than chasing after her."

She smiled at his humor. "Seth was wondering if you could find the swarm again and point it out to him. If the swarm is of honeybees, he'd like to give them a hive to live in."

James started to answer but paused to look at the picture Abby held up to him. He complimented her on finding one of trees bright with autumn colors, then waited while she let Leah see the page.

He hid his shock that his daughter was seeking out Leah as if they'd known each other for years.

He waited until his daughter was busy turning pages again before he answered Leah. There was nothing wrong with Abby's hearing, and he didn't want her to get upset about the bees. The hesitation gave him time to compose himself before Leah glanced in his direction again.

"I can understand your neighbor Seth's concern, because honeybees are disappearing. Nobody seems to know why, but we need to take care of the ones we have." He kept his voice low as he went on, "I'd be glad to take your friend to where we saw the swarm. However. . ." He glanced toward Abby and watched Leah do the same. "I'm not going to take her near the swarm again unless she wants to go." He grimaced. "I doubt that'll happen."

"Seth's Grossdawdi Perry assured us this morning that bees are less likely to sting while swarming. They're intent on finding a new home, so they shouldn't pay any attention to us unless we get close to the swarm."

"You and I can understand that, but I think it'd be better for her to stay here. I'm sure Myra won't mind. She's been a good friend to us. When she heard about the termites at our house, she insisted we stay here."

"So you live in Stony Brook?"

He nodded. "A few streets from here. We bought a fixer-upper with plans to fix it up." He smiled when Leah grinned at his inadvertent play on words. "I'm hoping when the termites are evicted, the walls can stand on their own."

---

Laughing with the Englischer, Leah was more baffled with every word James spoke. She was unsure why the owner of the bed-and-breakfast would care one way or the other if the little girl stayed there while James went to look at the bees. Was there a reason his wife was unable to watch over her own Kind? Many Englisch women worked outside the house, so Abby's *Mamm* might not be able to take care of Abby while James showed Seth where the swarm was. And if he was concerned about his daughter's opinion about the bees, why didn't he just ask Abby? The little girl was old enough to know her mind.

She was missing something. Something important.

But what?

Leah began, "If you ask Abby—"

Any remnants of humor left James's face. "Leah, I should have told you this right away. My daughter hasn't spoken in almost a year."

"Oh." She wished she could think of something to say, but she wasn't sure what. The idea that the Kind never spoke was disturbing.

"Most people ask at this point why she doesn't talk."

"I'm curious, of course, but I don't want to pry."

"You aren't prying. It's not as if it's a secret. Anyone she meets soon realizes Abby doesn't speak. She hasn't said anything since her mother died."

Leah managed not to gasp. Abby's Mamm was dead? Just as shocking was how James spoke of his wife's death as if it had no more importance than yesterday's weather.

She quickly realized she was mistaken. When he refused to meet her eyes, she realized his wife's death had shaken him deeply. He must have learned in the past year to deal with any questions by confronting her death head-on. Her Daed had raised similar walls when her own Mamm had died.

She looked at Abby. The poor, sweet Kind!

And poor James. To be left a widower with a traumatized Kind was a double blow. She sought words to offer him sympathy, but the first ones that came to mind were focused on Abby.

"I understand," Leah whispered, "how painful it is to lose one's Mamm at a young age. I wasn't much older than Abby when my Mamm died." Though her Daed and Grossmammi had tried to help, an emptiness remained in Leah's heart whenever she thought of Mamm.

"I'm sorry."

"Danki." Rising, she said, "You can let Seth know when you can get together with him to show him where the swarm is. I know he's eager to find it. He would have come today himself if he wasn't under the weather."

"I will." James stood. "As soon as I can arrange for a sitter for Abby, I'll get in touch with Seth. It may take a couple of days. Maybe Dorcas will watch her." He sighed. "I hate to ask her because she's so busy taking care of the bed-and-breakfast while Myra is away."

"I know you don't know me, but I can watch Abby while you show Seth where the bees are." She wanted to take back the words as soon as she spoke them. Was she out of her mind?

"You'd do that?" James asked, surprised.

Leah could think of a dozen reasons to say no, including her interest in learning more about the classes James taught. College wasn't something an Amish woman should think about. The Amish way was to finish eight years of schooling and become a part of the adult community. Studying a subject on one's own was permissible, however, especially if the knowledge was useful to the Leit as her herbal studies were.

And she still wasn't sure whether Ruth actually needed her help or just desired her company. Until she had answers to that, she should be careful about making other commitments. Yet Ruth had made it clear that Seth capturing the bees was important to her. Why? Another question without an answer.

It'd be wiser to tell James that she really couldn't help him, but she wouldn't lie. She had a heart-deep sympathy for the little girl. Just the sight of Abby's suffering, as well as James's, brought back memories of those grief-filled days after her Mamm's death. If Leah could ease even a moment of that grief, how could she turn her back on the troubled Kind?

So while her mind was busy listing all the reasons she should use his question as a graceful excuse to take back her offer, she listened to her heart, which was aching over the sorrow shared by James and his daughter.

"I'd be glad to watch her whenever I can."

# 4

Leah was washing the breakfast dishes the next morning when the back door opened and three women walked in, chattering like a flock of chickens. They appeared to be around Grossmammi's age, because the hair beneath their Kapps ranged in shades from dull gray to brilliant white.

Two of the women were short and so thin they looked emaciated, and the other woman, who was almost as round as she was tall, dwarfed her companions. Leah thought she might be taller than James, who had to be over six feet tall—and whom Leah couldn't seem to get out of her thoughts.

As she had before—to no effect—Leah reminded herself it was foolish to let thoughts of the Englischer loiter in her mind. Had she been wrong to offer to watch Abby? No, James needed help, and Leah had the time to assist, since it was clear that Grossmammi wasn't ill as her letter had suggested. Still, there must be some reason for her words, which had convinced both Leah and her Daed that the old woman needed help. Leah planned to stay for at least another few weeks, just to be certain that her Grossmammi was as hale as she acted. Perhaps seeing James again during that time would dim her fascination with him.

She focused on the three women. Each carried a straw basket over one arm and a dark purse over the other. As they regarded her with candid curiosity, Leah was startled to discover the slender women were so identical she wondered how anyone told them apart. They wore matching dark-green dresses, while the round woman wore a dress of the same design in a lush purple. Did one twin—for they must be twins—have more freckles? Was the other one's nose a bit humped, as if it'd been broken long ago?

"You must be Leah," the heavyset woman crowed.

Drying her hands on the towel hanging from a rod by the sink, Leah nodded. "I am."

"I knew it was you," the more-freckled twin said. "You've no idea how much Ruth has been anticipating your arrival."

"She's been counting the days." The other twin pointed to the calendar hanging on the door to the laundry room. "See? She marked off each day until you got here. I hope you plan on staying for a while."

"Ja," said the first twin. "Poor Ruth has been feeling lonely."

"We told her that she should move back to Pennsylvania to be with her family."

Leah opened her mouth, but she didn't get a chance to speak as the twins continued their conversation like a bizarre game of volleyball.

"Will she listen to us?" asked the freckled twin who had spoken first. "No! She says she's staying here, even if she's lonely."

"Is that any way to live? I ask you. Is it?"

"She—"

"Ida Mae! Vera Jean!" said the plump woman. "You're doing it again! You promised you wouldn't overwhelm this dear Kind with your comments and questions." Before they could say anything more, she turned to Leah. "You'll get used to them."

The women put their baskets on the table and drew aside the cloths on top before lifting out plates topped with cookies, slices of pie, and a container of what looked like Amish church spread. The mixture of marshmallow crème and peanut butter lathered on fresh bread was a favorite, especially with Kinder.

Leah watched, uncertain what to do as the women, whom she

assumed were Grossmammi's friends, went to the cupboards and took out plates and cups. One of the twins—Leah had no idea if she was Ida Mae or Vera Jean—turned on a burner after shaking the teakettle to determine how much water was in it.

As they were about to sit, the door opened. Leah doubted she'd ever been happier to see her Grossmammi.

"You're early," Ruth announced.

"You're late," countered the heavy woman with a smile. "So we started with the help of your granddaughter."

"They brought a feast," Leah said, gesturing toward the table. She edged closer to Grossmammi and lowered her voice. "These are your friends, ain't so?"

Instead of answering her, Ruth asked, "You didn't tell Leah your names?" She rolled her eyes as if she were a teenager. "What am I going to do with the three of you?" Pointing to the full-figured woman, she said, "Leah, this is my *gut* friend Naomi Byler. The other two are her cousins and also my *gut* friends, Ida Mae and Vera Jean Mast."

Grossmammi indicated which name belonged to which twin. Ida Mae was the one with extra freckles, while Vera Jean had the bump on her nose.

"These," Grossmammi continued, "are my dearest friends in Stony Brook, though why they'd expect you to be able to read their minds and know that is beyond me."

Naomi laughed. "We were about to get to the introductions." Sitting at the table, the pudgy woman motioned for Leah to join her. "My niece Dorcas mentioned that she met you."

"Ja," Leah said, "we had a nice chat when I stopped at the bed-and-breakfast yesterday."

The older women exchanged a glance, and their message couldn't be missed. They were wondering why she'd gone to the Englisch business.

Before she could explain, Grossmammi said, "She was doing an errand for Perry's grandson. Seth is eager to find the swarm of bees James Holden and his daughter saw in the woods."

"Did you get accurate directions?" asked Naomi.

"James said he would show Seth where the swarm is. Do you think that will be okay with Seth?"

"I'm sure it will be." Ruth patted her hand and smiled. "Seth was irked at not being able to speak with the Englischer himself, so he'll be grateful for any help. Will James be able to show him before the bees take off again?"

"He seemed ready to help. Seth can find him at the bed-and-breakfast. James said he and his daughter would be there for a few more days while they wait for their house in Stony Brook to be sprayed. They've got termites."

The women made the appropriate sounds of dismay.

"He's hoping," Leah went on, "that once they're home, his daughter won't have any more nightmares about the bees."

"Ach, James Holden's poor little daughter." Ruth sighed.

The other three women sighed too, and then Ida Mae said, "What a sad situation! The poor little lamb. Did she say anything to you, Leah?"

"Nothing. James said she hasn't spoken a word since her Mamm died. I know how I missed my Mamm after she passed away. I think I can help Abby. I agreed to babysit her when James needs someone. She seems to like me, or at least James thinks so."

Again Ruth patted Leah's hand. "Connie Holden's death was different from your Mamm's. There are many questions about what happened."

Leah's hand froze over the sugar bowl as she looked at the women. They avoided her eyes. "What do you mean?"

The older women shot uneasy glances at each other.

"Leah," Ruth said, "you need to know what's been said about Connie Holden's death. I didn't realize you'd offered to watch the Kind. I can't tell you how much of what's been whispered in Stony Brook is true and how much isn't." She set her cup on the table. "People have been saying that the car accident that caused Connie Holden's death wasn't an accident."

Leah wondered if she'd forgotten how to breathe. The air in her lungs seemed stuck, and she couldn't push it out or pull in another breath.

*Not an accident?*

That was the same as saying it had happened on purpose. If it had happened on purpose, someone had caused it.

But who?

Certainly not James Holden, who'd been so kind when he thought his daughter might have hurt her in Abby's rush to escape the bees, who'd inquired about Grossmammi's health, and who'd been embarrassed when he believed he hadn't asked quickly enough.

Somehow she managed to say, "I can't believe James Holden would do anything to his wife."

"Nobody believes he had anything to do with the awful accident that left him a widower with a young, mute daughter." Ruth's voice trailed away.

"Why would anyone think it wasn't an accident?" Leah prompted, wondering what was so horrible that Grossmammi couldn't bring herself to say the words.

Vera Jean said, "There's talk that his wife intentionally drove into the tree, even though Abby was in the car with her."

"She was ill," Ida Mae explained in not much more than a whisper. "It's said she couldn't face the pain."

"Why would a Mamm intentionally risk her little girl's life?" Leah asked.

Ruth sighed. "We'll never know whether Connie Holden was at fault or something went wrong with the car. We know God was looking out for Abby, because she was able to get out of the car unhurt. One thing I do know. You must be careful not to believe you can cure the Kind and her Daed. What they've suffered isn't anything healing herbs can help."

"I know." Leah tried not to sound miffed at how Grossmammi chided her as if she were no older than Abby.

Had Grossmammi sensed the content of Leah's prayers since her visit to the bed-and-breakfast? She'd asked God to help the Holdens. What she knew might be insufficient, but she believed God's love was enough to make the impossible possible.

---

James pulled his truck into the lane leading to the Eicher farm two days after he'd spoken with Leah at the bed-and-breakfast. He was there to talk to Seth Eicher about locating the swarm of honeybees. Leah had offered to babysit for him, but she hadn't given him a way to contact her. He should have asked, but he'd been distracted by the birdlike motions of her hands and her expressive face that revealed her thoughts before she spoke them.

Putting Leah out of his head was an arduous chore. He'd push thoughts of her aside, but the moment he let his mind wander, her image reappeared. She had a big heart; otherwise, she wouldn't have offered to be his backup babysitter. He couldn't believe he'd accepted when he hardly knew her.

But Abby responded to Leah.

If there was the slightest chance Leah could be the key to unlocking

Abby's silent world, he must not let the opportunity slip away.

The truck bounced in a pothole, and James gripped the wheel. Guilt bit into him when he glanced into the rearview mirror and saw Abby sitting in her car seat. She was looking out the window at the cornfield beside the road. Before she could catch him staring at her, he looked back at the narrow farm lane.

He shouldn't have brought Abby with him, but he couldn't find anyone for her to stay with in Stony Brook after his usual babysitter canceled at the last minute. Without a phone at the Kauffman farm, he refused to show up there and ask Leah to watch Abby. That wouldn't be fair to either of them. Instead he planned to talk to Seth about helping him find the swarm in a day or two. That would give him time to make arrangements with Leah to watch Abby.

The Eichers' white farmhouse was much like others surrounding Stony Brook. What it must have looked like when it was first built had been lost in the additions that stuck out in every direction. He was less impressed by the house than the massive spruce in the front yard. It would have taken at least a century for a tree to obtain such a prodigious height.

He parked the truck by a shed. Getting out, he lifted Abby from her seat. He didn't say anything when she clung to him. Maybe the beekeeper would have honey he could buy. That might ease his daughter's fears.

James was startled to see two people walking toward him. He gave the Amish man a quick glance as the man bent toward the woman, clearly asking her a question. She nodded and kept walking toward James. The man, who had light brown hair, turned and hurried back in the direction they'd come. Had James done something wrong before uttering a single word?

Then James recognized the woman who had been talking to the Amish man.

"Leah?" he asked, surprised.

"Gute Mariye." She looked as shocked as he felt that they were both at the Eicher farm at the same time.

"I didn't expect to see you here this morning."

"My Grossmammi sent me over with some bread she'd baked." She faltered. "Are you here about the bees? I didn't think you'd bring Abby along for that."

"My babysitter had to cancel."

"But I said I would be glad to—" She glanced over her shoulder and didn't say anything more as the Amish man rushed toward them, carrying something white over one arm.

James was puzzled. Was the man she was with Seth Eicher? Could she be trying to hide from her neighbor the fact that she'd agreed to watch his daughter? It wouldn't be a problem for her among the other Amish, would it? Dorcas had sat for him at the bed-and-breakfast, and she hadn't acted as if there was anything wrong with her doing that.

Leah quickly introduced James to the other man.

Seth gave him a terse greeting. He clearly didn't want to wait any longer to capture the bees. He shook out the white fabric from over his arm. It was a beekeeper's safety suit. He had attached a helmet with a veiled faceplate that he could set on his head. He carried a small metal pot with a handle and a spout that let out of a wisp of smoke in one hand. He walked around the truck and picked up a large slab of wood. He balanced it on his shoulder.

"Bring the supers," he said as he began walking toward the woods.

"Supers?" asked James.

Leah pointed to a trio of wooden boxes. "Supers are stacked together to form a beehive."

"I'll carry them."

She nodded and held out her arms to Abby. "We'll wait here."

As soon as he'd handed his daughter to her, James picked up the wooden boxes. He was glad he could hide his continuing shock at how Abby showed more emotion with Leah than anyone else, even him.

Leah set the little girl on her feet. Abby grasped Leah's hand and gazed at her. James waited for any sign of a smile, but his daughter's expression remained somber. He remembered when she'd been a toddler, chortling over something or screaming if she didn't get her way. He'd hated that shrieking, but he'd give almost anything to hear it again.

"We'll be fine, James," Leah said. "Go ahead with Seth."

Before he could answer, Abby grabbed onto his belt.

"Stay with Leah," James said. "I'll be right back after I show Seth where the bees are."

Abby looked at Leah and shook her head.

Leah said, "He'll be fine. Seth knows how to handle the bees. You don't need to worry about your dad."

Again Abby shook her head. She tugged on Leah's hand while still gripping James's belt.

There was disbelief in Leah's voice when she said, "I think she wants to go with you, and she wants me to come too."

"Why would she want to do that?" *And how do you understand my daughter better than I do?*

"I don't know," she replied, "but we need to get going so we don't lose sight of Seth among the trees."

"He should have waited for me to show him where to go," James said. "I thought he needed my help."

"He figured we wouldn't stand around jawing if he headed out." Her smile returned when she looked at Abby. "Komm! Let's enjoy our walk. I'll show you a few of my favorite plants."

James followed them, toting the boxes containing the wooden frames. He assumed they helped the bees create a new honeycomb.

How could he figure that out, but had no idea what was going on with Leah? Had he insulted her? She was as standoffish as if they were strangers.

*We* are *strangers*, he reminded himself. Despite their meeting on the road and the one companionable conversation they'd had at the Maple Shade Bed and Breakfast, they lived in two different worlds. He was a modern Mennonite who drove a pickup truck, had a cell phone and a microwave, and was working on his PhD. She was a conservative Amish woman who kept her head covered, drove a buggy, and hadn't gone to school past the eighth grade.

Those facts listed the cold truth, but they didn't include how Abby had responded to Leah. He wished he knew why.

What was it about Leah Kauffman that spoke to his daughter's heart?

It couldn't be because Leah reminded Abby of her mother. Leah's hair was as dark as midnight, while Connie had worn her pale blonde hair in a shaggy, carefree style. While Leah dressed plainly, Connie had loved chunky jewelry and silver rings, which she wore on almost every finger, except the one on which she wore the simple gold wedding band he'd given her. Connie had preferred musky perfume, and the only scents from Leah seemed to be from a flowery shampoo and a sensible soap.

He passed Leah, who was pointing out a low ground cover to his daughter. Neither of them glanced in his direction, so he hurried to catch up with Seth and led the way toward the place where they'd seen the bees.

The low buzz from the bees helped James pinpoint the swarm.

Seth adjusted everything, setting the supers on flat stones raised closer to the swarm that vibrated with the motion of the bees. He reached to pull his helmet over his head, but glanced past James to where Leah stood about ten feet away with Abby.

"I need you to stay there and be quiet." He glanced at Abby. "Will she be quiet if the bees start flying around?"

James nodded. When Abby had fled the bees, she hadn't made a sound other than her sneakers slapping the ground.

Leah released Abby's hand and went to the other man. She whispered something to Seth. Though he didn't hear the words, James knew she must have told him how Abby had been mute for the past year. In him swelled an instinct too primitive to name. It urged him to defend his child, saying nothing was wrong with her, that she could talk again whenever she chose.

*If only that were true.*

Once he might have murmured a prayer for God to have mercy on Abby and help her heal, but God hadn't listened to any of James's prayers in far too long. Maybe the Almighty had other matters that demanded His attention. Maybe James's flagging faith—which had weakened soon after the death of Brian, his best friend during college—proved that he was unworthy of asking God's grace upon what remained of his family.

He went with Leah to where Abby was standing, her eyes wide as they watched Seth.

The beekeeper raised the uppermost box higher, so it wasn't far below the swarm. As if they'd asked, he explained that the super needed to be as close as possible to the swarm. If there was too much space between the bees and what would be their new home, the bees could fly away without realizing that what they sought was right below them.

James tensed when Seth slapped his hand against the branch next to the swarm. He relaxed as he watched the bees tumble into the super.

More quickly than he would have guessed possible, the majority of the bees were ensconced in the supers. When Seth set the board on top, a few bees flew around the tree where hundreds had been minutes before.

Abby grabbed onto James's belt again, and he felt her trembling.

"It's okay," he reassured his daughter. "Seth is going to make sure the bees are happy so they won't sting anyone. Isn't that right?"

---

As Seth said a distracted, "Ja," Leah knelt beside Abby. Why couldn't Seth be more reassuring? She'd explained to him about how frightened Abby had been. Recalling that Seth lived with an old man and a younger brother, she knew he might not have realized the impact his words would have on the Kind.

"I know you don't like bees much now, Abby," Leah said, "but we need to be grateful to God for His wisdom. He knew how we would love flowers, so He gave us bees to help the flowers grow."

The little girl stared at her as if Leah had lost her mind.

"No, really," Leah said, trying not to laugh. Abby could make herself understood when she wanted to.

Should Leah respond to her when Abby didn't speak? Not answering or refusing to talk herself until the little girl did seemed cruel. Punishing the Kind for something that wasn't her fault was wrong.

Bidding Seth goodbye and doubting he heard her because he was fixated on the bees, Leah walked with the Holdens toward their truck. She told Abby about the autumn flowers they passed and swung their hands between them.

James opened his truck's back door and buckled Abby into her seat. He closed the door and faced Leah. "Thank you for talking to her as if she's talking back."

"She is, just not with her voice. I can guess what she's thinking by her expression or how she moves her hands or her stance."

"You can?" He didn't bother to hide his amazement.

"Can't you? You Englischers have a name for it. Body language, ain't so?"

"That's right, but I'm not good at understanding it. I can read the heart of a tree by looking at how it's growing or the health of its leaves, but I can't figure out what my own daughter has on her mind."

"You know her better than anyone else. Observe her, and you'll be able to discern her thoughts too. At least sometimes."

"Will you teach me?"

She hesitated before answering, remembering Ruth's warning not to assume she could heal the Englisch family.

But how could she deny him the chance to reach his Kind?

"Ja," she said, hoping she could make her Grossmammi understand.

# 5

The sun was up when Leah opened her eyes the next morning. She was shocked that she'd slept late.

Or that she'd slept at all.

She sat up, leaning one shoulder against the simple headboard on the double bed where she'd tossed and turned most of the night, thinking about how she could teach James to read Abby's physical reactions. She had sympathy for both Daed and daughter. James couldn't be unaware of the whispers in Stony Brook about his wife's death. Had Abby heard them too?

The faint gold-pink of the morning light sifted around the dark-green shade on the room's single window to brighten the white walls. Under Leah's bare toes was a rag rug. She dug her toes into its seams.

She looked at the books on the shelf beside the window. She wasn't sure why Grossmammi had books for Kinder upstairs in her guest room, but the bright bindings looked pretty on the shelf.

Today James was bringing Abby to the farm for the first time. Would the little girl be willing to stay, or would she resist when her Daed started to leave?

James had admitted he didn't have any idea what was going on in his daughter's head. She'd seen how his lips pursed, the corners pinched to white, when he tried to hide his frustration with being unable to break through Abby's silence.

Why did Leah think she'd do any better with the wounded Kind?

*Lord, I'm going to need Your help today. There is no herb I know of that will persuade Abby to talk again. You know what's in her heart, and You know what lies ahead for her, as You do for each of us. If I can ease her way along the path You've set for her, show me the way.*

Her prayer didn't include all her petitions because she yearned to know the truth about James's wife's death. She wondered if Dorcas might have more information about the rumors.

Leah smiled as she recalled how her new friend had said Aenti Naomi, Grossmammi Ruth, and the twins were the best source of information in the county. That was true when it came to the Amish, but Leah couldn't be certain how connected they were to gossip among the Englischers. It wouldn't hurt to find out what Dorcas knew.

Feeling better after she'd said her prayer and made a plan, Leah dressed and went downstairs to find Ruth making bread. The aroma of bacon drew Leah in, and, greeting Ruth, she went to the stove and served herself scrambled eggs, fried potatoes, and bacon that were being kept warm in cast-iron skillets.

"I'm sorry I overslept," Leah said as she poured herself a cup of pungent coffee and carried the cup and her plate to the table.

"You don't need to apologize." Grossmammi smiled. "Eat your breakfast and enjoy it. I like having someone else to cook for." Not giving Leah a chance to reply, she asked, "What do you have planned for today?"

"Making us dinner and supper." She savored the eggs, which were flavored with dried thyme and cilantro from Grossmammi's herb garden. "I'm also going to be watching Abby Holden today."

The older woman looked over her shoulder. "I don't think that is a *gut* idea." She rubbed her hands together, letting flour fall on the counter.

"I can help, so shouldn't I?"

"Helping within the community is one thing, but this . . ." She shook her head. "You're new to Stony Brook, and the Leit doesn't know you."

"I've met your friends and Dorcas and the Eichers. That's a large portion of the district."

"True, there are no more than fifty of us." Grossmammi started kneading the dough, harder than was necessary, showing how distressed she was.

Rising and walking over to stand beside Ruth, Leah said, "Watching Abby is an occasional thing when James can't find another babysitter. How could I say no when his daughter seems to like me?"

"Do you like her?"

"Ja, she's a sweet Kind."

"Is it only the daughter you like?"

Shocked, Leah stared at Ruth before looking away. Her astonishment wasn't at the question, but at her own reaction to it. She couldn't help admiring James. Not just for his *gut* looks, but because of how deeply he loved his daughter and his determination to reach her again. In addition, she was fascinated with the fact he was a teacher in a field she wanted to learn more about.

"James isn't Amish." Leah sat at the table. "Grossmammi, why did you send me that letter suggesting you needed help?"

"I do need help, and you're being a great one." The older woman didn't look at her. "It was a blessing not to have to do the laundry on my own this week."

"Thank God you aren't ill."

"I never said I was. I wished you'd come to visit, and now you're here. Aren't you glad? You've met my neighbors, and I hope you'll want to get to know them better. I know they want to learn more about you and make you feel welcome in Stony Brook."

When Ruth smiled, Leah pushed down the rebellious thoughts bubbling into her mind. No matter what Ruth said, Leah guessed her Grossmammi had had a specific aim in writing that letter.

Leah wished she knew what it was.

An hour later, James's red pickup slowed in front of the round barn Leah had yet to explore. Maybe she'd take Abby into the barn and see if there were any kittens. Leah couldn't imagine a Kind who could resist playing with a rambunctious litter.

Leah waited until James and his daughter were out of the truck. "Welcome to my Grossmammi's farm." She smiled brightly, but Abby regarded her without expression.

"We're glad you can spend time with Abby today," James said.

"I've been looking forward to it. I thought Abby could assist me with my chores. I need to help Grossmammi do garden work. It's harvesttime now." She didn't let her smile slide away. "We'll have a *gut* time."

Abby walked away to look at the mums planted by the porch.

James sighed.

"She'll be fine here," Leah said.

"I know," he replied. "I'd hoped when she saw you again . . ." He released another sigh. "You're the first one she's made eye contact with since the accident."

Did he believe his wife's death was an accident, or did he have suspicions like the rumors whispered through Stony Brook? Maybe neither, Leah realized with a start. He might know the truth, though he hadn't said anything to her.

Knowing she couldn't ask, she said, "I know you don't want to hear this, but have patience."

"I have had patience." His voice was sharp, and he flushed. "I'm sorry, Leah. I know you're trying to help." He held out a small sheet of paper. "Here's my cell number. Call if you have any problems. You don't have a phone, though, do you?"

"Grossmammi shares one with the Eichers. Don't worry. We won't have any problems, I'm sure, but danki. And James, I trust that God will bring healing to Abby's heart." She put her hand on his arm before she could stop herself.

She jerked her fingers away as a shocking warmth leaped from his skin to hers. Clasping her hands in front of her, she backed away.

James opened his mouth to say something, but muttered only a faint "Goodbye" before he climbed into his truck and drove away.

Leah released the stale air in her lungs, wondering how long she'd been holding her breath. She needed to be careful not to be drawn in by her undeniable attraction to James Holden.

Crossing the yard to where Abby was staring at the flowers, Leah said, "I'm going to the barn. Would you like to see inside?"

No answer.

"Well, I would!" Leah tried to keep her voice cheerful. "I've never been in a round barn like this one, and I can't wait to see inside it." She held out her hand. "Let's go. Who knows what we might find?"

She was relieved when Abby put her small fingers on Leah's palm. With a smile, as if she'd never doubted Abby would take her hand, Leah shortened her stride to match the child's as they walked toward the barn.

They strolled through the round barn with its amazing pattern of rafters and the center support reaching to the roof, like a giant sculpture of a tree. Not even a litter of playful kittens drew a smile from Abby. Leah thought of her cousins who were around Abby's age. They never could have been so still or not uttered a single word in the past hour.

Or in a year.

A shiver ran icy fingers down her spine. Thinking of Abby shutting herself off from the rest of the world made Leah want to weep.

It might have been easier if Leah hadn't lost her own mother as a child. She remembered the anguish and the longing to disbelieve what everyone was telling her—that Mamm was in a much better place and would be waiting for her. Daed wouldn't have lied to her. Nor would have their bishop, who always had a gentle word for the Kinder, even when they weren't able to sit quietly during the lengthy Sunday service.

Being surrounded by a loving community who had stepped in to make sure she, her siblings, and her Daed had warm meals and a clean house and no need to worry about any of the chores being done had helped. When Leah had needed to talk or cry or be held, someone had always been there. She'd found solace in knowing her Daed and siblings had the same support.

Abby had sealed herself away in an invisible bubble where she could be seen yet not interact with the rest of the world. There must be some way to pop that bubble and free her, but Leah didn't have any idea how.

James had tried, she knew, and if he couldn't reach his daughter, why did she think she could?

*Because I have You to help me, God.* The prayer rose from her heart, a prayer for both James and his daughter to find relief from their sorrow.

Leading the little girl to the garden, Leah gave her a smile. "I noticed the rows of beans could use weeding and harvesting. Do you want to help me?"

The little girl stared at her, shifting from foot to foot.

"Don't worry," Leah said. "I'll show you which plants are weeds. After we get a bucket of beans, we can sample a few. There's nothing better than fresh vegetables right out of the garden, ain't so?"

Abby nodded.

Leah wanted to shout her happiness at getting a response. Instead, she took two buckets from the back porch and led the little girl into the garden. Abby was distracted for a moment by the pumpkins that were beginning to turn orange. She worked beside Leah, seeming to take comfort from the simple tasks.

When Leah pulled out a thick clump of weeds, she saw the sunlight reflecting off a moist body. She pulled a worm from the ground.

It was long, and she set it on her dirty left palm. Tapping Abby on the shoulder, she said, "Look at this."

The little girl did, and her eyes got big.

"Worms are a gardener's *gut* friends," she said as the worm wiggled across her palm, trying to find a way to escape. "Do you know why?"

Abby shook her head.

"Can you guess?"

The little girl shook her head again.

Leah considered asking another question that couldn't be answered with a yes or no, but she didn't want to undo the camaraderie she was establishing with Abby. It wasn't much, but it was far more than she'd had a few minutes ago.

"A worm loves to dig through the dirt, and when he digs, he leaves a little tunnel behind him. Of course, dirt falls in after he passes, but some of the spaces he leaves fill with air and water, waiting for a plant's roots. Because the plant doesn't have to work so hard to spread its roots, it can grow bigger above ground and give us vegetables and fruits." Leah smiled as she bounced the worm to the center of her hand. "Would you like to hold it?"

Abby shook her head and drew back.

"Why don't you touch him? He feels like when you dig your fingers into the damp ground."

The little girl put a tentative finger out, and Leah moved the worm beneath it. Abby pulled back, then stroked the worm a single time. She folded her hands in a clear announcement that touching the worm once was enough.

Leah placed the worm on the ground and watched as it burrowed out of sight. Abby agreeing to do as Leah had asked wasn't a big thing, but it had been another step in the right direction.

She hoped it was the first of many more to come.

---

James wiped sweat off one palm and then the other as he drove toward the Kauffman farm. He'd been a waste during his classes today. Instead of keeping to his lesson plan and answering his students' questions, he'd spent the whole time pondering how Leah and Abby were doing.

Others had offered to watch Abby, and he'd known they wanted to help his daughter overcome her trauma. Most of them had given up after a short time. He didn't want Leah to be another name on that list, especially since she seemed to be making progress.

What if it had fallen apart today?

When he stopped near the farmhouse, he saw Leah and Abby sitting on the porch steps. Making sure he had a cheerful smile on his face, James got out of the truck. His expression became genuine when Leah waved to him . . . and Abby did too. When was the last time his daughter had acknowledged his return home?

Leah brought Abby over to the truck. She waited while he set his daughter in her car seat before telling Abby to come again soon.

Did she have any idea how those simple, trite words sent his heart soaring like a joyous balloon?

His smile as he closed the back door was genuine. "Everything went well?"

"As well as it could." Leah glanced at Abby who was looking at a book. "We had a good time together in the garden. I know God holds Abby in His hands, and He'll bring her healing and peace when He knows the time is right. He's there for us every minute of our lives, not only in our times of need. We're never alone."

James nodded so he didn't have to speak. Anything he said would show how he wished he had the faith she possessed. It was as much a part of her as her silky black hair and her warm brown eyes.

He once had lived his faith, but it began to die when his best friend had been killed fighting in the Middle East a few months before Abby was born. Connie's death last year had raised an even higher wall between him and God, a wall he didn't know how to dismantle. Some days he wasn't even sure he wanted to tear it down. Hiding behind anger and frustration, he didn't have to give into grief.

Was that why Abby hid in silence?

Wrestling that painful thought into the recesses of his mind, he asked, "So I can bring Abby again?"

"Of course."

"Is tomorrow too soon? I need to go and meet with my advisor at Miami University. We meet every Friday."

When she hesitated before answering, he wondered if he was putting her into a difficult situation. He knew the Amish wished to be separate from the rest of the world.

A throat was cleared behind him, and he glanced over his shoulder to see Ruth Kauffman. She wore a smile as strained as his own had been when he arrived at the farm. That, he knew, was not a good thing.

Leah saw the look exchanged by James and Ruth, but she acted as if she hadn't. "Of course," she repeated. "I'd be delighted to watch

Abby tomorrow." Stepping away from the truck, she said, "I've got more weeding to do, and she was a great help today."

"It's nice to see you again, James," Ruth said before giving Leah a taut smile. "You should clean up. Seth is joining you for supper." She glanced in James's direction. "I asked Dorcas too, so it's not you and Seth alone."

"Alone?" Leah was astonished. "Aren't you having supper with us?"

"No. I go out on Thursday evenings."

"Where are you going?"

"To see my friends." She smiled as she drew her black bonnet from behind her and tied it beneath her chin. "Ida Mae, Vera Jean, Naomi, and I get together each week on Thursday."

"Oh, that sounds like fun."

"We do have fun together."

"Are you going to the Masts' house or Naomi's?"

Instead of answering, Ruth said, "If I don't leave now, I'll be late."

Leah stepped aside before the older woman walked right over her. Ruth strode along the farm lane like someone half her age.

"Is your grandmother always so evasive?" James asked.

"No," Leah answered with a frown.

*What is going on? First the odd letter, and now this odder behavior. What is Grossmammi hiding?*

# 6

James's pickup stopped between the house and the barn the next morning while Leah was spreading corn for the chickens. Looking over her shoulder, she smiled when she saw James step from the truck. He opened the back door and reached in. Moments later he swung his daughter out and set her on the ground.

Leah strained her ears. Any other child would have laughed or squealed with glee. James's daughter didn't make a sound.

Abby, however, looked around with keen interest, and Leah guessed the little girl was eager to continue her exploration of the farm. When Abby pointed toward something on the front yard, James bent to answer her unuttered question.

The sight brought forth the tears that seemed to lurk nearby whenever Leah considered what James and his daughter had to deal with each day. She was sure he'd done everything he could—including seeking advice from plenty of medical experts—to encourage Abby to speak and smile again.

Nothing had worked.

So why did she continue to believe she could help the Kind? *Because I know You're with me, God. I want to be the instrument of Your healing for a little girl's heart. And her Daed's.*

Again shock whipped through her. She needed to heed Grossmammi. Helping James by watching Abby was one thing, but she must not see herself as a long-term venue through which God could work His changes. She was Amish, and they weren't.

Or she would be truly Amish once she took classes in preparation for being baptized and becoming a full member of the Leit. She'd postponed the classes she'd intended to take with four friends back in Pennsylvania. The five of them had spent most of their lives together. They'd been scholars at the same one-room schoolhouse, and they'd shared eight years of end-of-the year exercises and Christmas programs. As they'd learned skills for taking care of a house or the farm animals, they'd shared the knowledge with each other. Leah had instructed her friends in what Ruth had taught her about herbs.

Now the other four were going to be baptized without her, but Leah didn't regret the delay. Right now her place was in Indiana where she could be with her Grossmammi. Last night Ruth had returned home long after dark. Leah was glad to help her get ready for bed and have her breakfast ready this morning when Ruth woke much later than usual.

Attempts Leah had made to get Ruth to explain what she'd been doing had been a waste of time. The older woman was tight-lipped, changing the subject each time Leah tried to bring up her late evening out. Instead Ruth had asked question after question about what Leah thought of Seth.

The honest answer was Leah thought Seth was a nice man. She told Ruth that, but she didn't add how boring Seth was when he talked on and on about his bees and the price of honey and the supers with the bees from the swarm James had found. Leah had pretended to be interested, but she was relieved when Dorcas had interjected anecdotes about the bed-and-breakfast whenever she could. If her new friend hadn't been there, Leah wasn't sure that she could have kept from nodding off during one of Seth's explanations.

James called a greeting, jerking her out of her memories of last evening's supper.

She waved to let him know she'd heard him and then carried the bucket of chicken feed toward the house. She pulled out a handful of feed before putting the top on the bucket to keep out squirrels and skunks. After setting the bucket in the storage closet on the back porch, she walked toward the Holdens.

James wore a navy coat over khaki trousers. A fanciful tie decorated with tiny cars fell over the front of his light-blue shirt. In contrast, he wore black sneakers that peeked out from beneath his pants.

She pulled her attention from him and looked at Abby. Like her father, she wore a dark-colored coat, but hers was over a pair of bright-pink top-and-pants outfit. Her sneakers had sparkles and were tied with striped aqua-and-white laces.

"Gute Mariye," Leah said as she reached them. "You look fancy this morning."

"I'm meeting with my advisor's peers to go over my latest research." James ran his fingers along the inside of his collar. "That's the only reason I ever willingly wear a tie. As soon as I'm done, it comes off."

Leah chuckled, then bent down so her eyes were even with Abby's. "Would you like to finish feeding the chickens for me?" She took the little girl's hand, cupped her fingers and poured the feed onto her palm.

Without a word, Abby walked over to where the chickens were pecking at the ground. Leah urged her to strew the feed, but the little girl began to toss the feed, one kernel at a time, toward the birds.

"Doesn't Abby go to school?" Leah asked as she stood up. "I thought Englisch kids started school when they were five."

"How can she go to school when she won't talk?" James's smile faded. "I've been working with her when I have the time, and she's writing her ABCs and doing simple arithmetic. I think she is reading as well, but without being able to ask her questions, I can't be certain if she's doing more than just looking at the pictures."

"Grossmammi has the basic books we use in Amish schools. If you'd like, I can share them with Abby when she's here. They're aimed at plain Kinder, but I doubt the stories are different from what's in Englisch school books."

"A great idea! I'm glad you came to Stony Brook, Leah."

Judging by the sudden heat in her cheeks, she guessed they were a fiery red, and she ducked her head. She shouldn't be pleased with his words. They probably only meant he was happy she was helping his daughter. She was amazed to discover how much she wished he was glad she was visiting because he appreciated her for more than helping his daughter.

*Don't go there*, she warned herself. *He's an Englischer, and you're Amish.*

Aloud she replied, "Compliments aren't the plain way."

"Okay," he said with a smile. "But it's *my* way to be grateful when someone helps my daughter."

So his words really had been about the time she spent with Abby. She should have been relieved, but a swell of disappointment flooded her.

"How's the termite situation coming?" Leah needed to change the subject to something less personal.

"Almost done," James replied. "I'm told we'll be able to move home in a couple of days. Not that I'm complaining. It'll be back to my own cooking, which doesn't compare to Dorcas's."

Leah made a mental note to send some of the sweet rolls rising in the kitchen home with Abby at the day's end.

"What are you planning for Abby today?" James asked.

"Seth invited me to visit his beehives so I can see how the bees you found are doing in their new home." She glanced toward where Abby was watching the chickens with wide eyes. "I thought I'd take her with me."

His expression hardened. "I'm not sure that's a good idea. She's still having bad dreams."

"Are you certain they're about the bees? She seemed interested when Seth was collecting the swarm."

He jammed his hands into his pockets. "Leah, I'm not certain about anything. All I know is she climbs in bed with me and weeps silently."

"You know I won't let her get stung." She had to fight her own instinct to reach out her hand to offer him comfort. "She'll see that the bees are under control. That might help with her nightmares."

He rubbed his fingers against his forehead and sighed. "Like I said, I can't tell if her nightmares are about the bees or something else."

"Did she have nightmares before the bees?"

"Yes." He seemed ready to add more on the subject but must have decided not to because his next words were, "You may be right. If she sees the bees are focused on making honey and don't have any interest in stinging her if she stays away from them, it could put one of her terrors to rest."

"If it's too much for her, I'll bring her back immediately."

"Good." He motioned toward his red truck. "Shall we go?"

"You're coming too? I thought you needed to see your advisor."

"I do, but I was going to get there early to spend time on my thesis. My meeting isn't for a couple of hours. If you don't mind, I'd like to see how our bees are doing."

"Okay." What else could she say? That he couldn't come with her? That would be rude.

Abby was his daughter, and James should be the judge of whether she should visit the hive. And Leah couldn't lie to herself. She liked the idea of spending a bit more time with this intriguing man.

"We can cut across the field." She glanced at his feet. "*Gut* thing you're wearing sneakers."

James went to get his daughter, and the three of them walked across the field between the two farms. It'd been left to pasture, so they had to wade through thick grass. He picked Abby up because the grass reached almost to her waist.

While they walked, Leah watched the little girl. Abby didn't need to speak for Leah to know she was leery of visiting the hives. While they crossed the field, Leah explained again how important the bees were to help the garden plants grow.

Seth was standing near his white hives when they came through the gate into the front yard. The six hives were set in front of a rickety barn Leah hadn't noticed before because it was set in the shadow of the big cow barn.

He looked up, surprised, when she and the Holdens walked toward him. "Gute Mariye," he called. "Good morning."

"We thought we'd see how the swarm is settling in." Leah glanced at the boxes where bees flew in and out, ignoring the humans.

"Oh, none of these are the bees from the swarm."

"Where are they?" James asked.

He crooked a finger and began to stride toward the tumbledown barn. He didn't look back to see if they were following as he went inside.

James arched a single brow, and Leah tried not to laugh. She understood what he didn't say. The barn looked unsteady enough that Abby could push it over with a single shove.

The barn was divided inside. The area they entered was small and almost lost to dusk. The windows were draped by dirt-encrusted spiderwebs, allowing very little sunlight to pass through the thick strands.

Leah squinted, trying to see through the shadows. She didn't want to blunder into the hive.

"The swarm is here," Seth said, pointing.

The supers were covered with an often-mended tarp that might once have been bright blue. It had faded to a dull gray, the same shade as the wooden floors.

"They need to stay in the dark," the beekeeper said, "until they forget the scent trails they used to follow. I'll keep them here for three or four more weeks before I move them outside. By that time, they'll be ready to find new routes to flowering plants."

"There won't be many flowers by then," Leah said.

"The chill will keep them in the hive, and I'll have to make sure the hive has enough sugar water until the bees can begin working in the spring. Once the weather is warm, they'll gather what they need to make their own food."

James walked around the covered hive, examining it from every angle. "That's fascinating. I'm glad you rescued the bees, Seth."

"Me too." He gave James a rare grin. "The extra hive will increase the amount of honey I can sell from now on. Danki for leading me to the swarm."

"What's on the other side of the barn?" James asked.

Seth shrugged. "You'd have to ask my Grossdawdi. I haven't gone in there in years. Grossdawdi has kept everything he's ever bought for the farm. Forty-five years' worth of accumulation. I'd guess it's filled with things rusting away."

"At least he's keeping the stuff out here and not in the house," Leah said.

Seth nodded. "Ja, you're right. I shouldn't forget to thank God for such small favors. Let me show you the active hives." Again he walked away, sure they'd trail after him like a line of ducklings.

Abby grabbed Leah's hand, startling her and James. His eyes widened when the little girl then took his hand.

Seth frowned when he turned to see the three of them linked

together, but Leah said nothing. She wasn't going to deny the little girl whatever comfort was available.

"You're brave to come and see the bees," Leah whispered to Abby as they walked out of the barn.

Abby nodded, but continued to stare at the hives.

"They're busy building their home and aren't the least bit interested in us." She put an arm around Abby's slender shoulders. "They want the chance to find flowers and collect the pollen and bring it to feed the others in the hive."

Abby halted.

Leah stopped too. "I think this is as close as Abby wants to get. Go ahead, James, and let Seth show you his hives. We'll wait here."

Though Leah would have liked to see inside the supers, she waited with Abby while James listened to Seth's explanation of how a hive worked—with the bees having a single goal of protecting their queen and her new offspring.

Noticing kittens on the house's porch, Leah urged Abby to go and see them. The little girl resisted for a moment, but then, when the hum of the bees grew stronger as Seth lifted the top off a hive, she scampered toward the house.

James asked plenty of questions, much to Seth's delight. When Leah noticed James glancing at his watch, she stepped forward.

"Danki, Seth, for showing us your hives. I think coming here has eased some of Abby's fear." She smiled. "At least enough so she won't flee in panic if she sees a swarm of bees again."

"I'm glad to help." His face softened as he glanced at his hives. "I appreciate the chance to save those honeybees, and they might have died if you and Abby hadn't stumbled upon them, James."

"Where is Abby?" James asked.

"With the kittens on the porch," Leah replied, gesturing to

where Abby was surrounded by multicolored kittens. Two were tigers, one ginger and the other gray. Another was black with two splotches of white on its front feet. A calico pounced on a white cat with a rust tip on its tail. The last one was covered with black and white patches.

The kittens wove around Abby, rubbing against her, eager for her attention. She petted each one before selecting the calico and holding it close to her face. The kitten's pink tongue flicked out to brush Abby's cheek.

James looked away, and Leah knew he had been hoping the kittens would make his daughter smile. His shoulders appeared weighed down by the grief he tried to keep hidden. Every inch of him revealed how burdened he was by his daughter's situation.

Though she had tried not to let Ruth's friends' comments lodge in her brain, she couldn't keep them away now. *Had James's wife tried to kill herself*—and *her Kind? If so, did James feel guilty for not catching signs of his wife's desperation?*

Those were questions she couldn't ask, but not knowing bothered her more and more.

"Showing off your pets, brother?" asked a deep voice from behind them.

Leah turned to see a stranger whom she assumed must be Willard Eicher. His hair was a similar color to his older brother's, but the resemblance ended there. His eyes were an almost colorless blue, and he boldly eyed her with as much interest as if she were a horse at an auction. He had a scar under his left eye and was missing the tip of the smallest finger on his left hand. She wondered if he'd hurt himself in a farm accident or playing as a boy.

"So you're Leah?" he asked in a tone that suggested he knew the answer.

She guessed he did. With a small community like Stony Brook, any newcomers were easy to identify.

"She and the Holdens came over," Seth said, showing he was also uncomfortable with his brother's brazen stare, "to see the bees they discovered a few days ago."

"Holdens?" Willard frowned at James. "I only see one."

"Abby is sitting on the porch, playing with the barn kittens."

"Kittens?" Glancing at the house, Seth's brother turned on his heel and strode away.

Leah stared after him, wondering why he'd acted like a dog was nipping at his heels. Out of the corner of her eye, she saw Seth's puzzled expression, and she realized he was just as baffled about his brother's retreat.

She wasn't confused about how she felt about Willard's ogling—it made her feel as if she were on display in a store window.

"Willard acts odd sometimes, but he's changed in the past six months or so. He started taking baptismal classes." Seth sounded flummoxed by his own words. "He's not the same as he was a year ago, though he still hangs out with his Englisch friends sometimes. Yet I can't always figure out why he does what he does."

"Like now?" James's voice was restrained. Not giving them a chance to answer, he said, "Come on, Leah. I'll walk you and Abby back to your grandmother's house."

He strode toward his daughter, leaving Leah to wonder if everyone had gone a bit mad in the last few seconds.

---

James tried to shove his reaction to the younger Eicher brother deep inside him so he could stop frowning. It might make Abby think he was upset with her. He wasn't. He was angry with himself. If a non-Amish man had gawked at Leah, James knew what he'd do: He'd tell the guy to keep his avid glances to himself. Instead he'd hesitated, not knowing how Leah and Seth would take his words. Would they view them as trying to provoke a fight? He didn't intend to do that, but he wanted the younger Eicher to treat Leah with respect.

Trying to believe the problem was none of his business, he couldn't convince himself. He was annoyed. The Eicher men could court Leah if they chose. That door was shut for James.

He started at the thought. Had he lost every bit of sense he'd ever had? If he wanted a relationship now—which he didn't because he needed to concentrate on his daughter and his studies—yearning for what he could never have would only add to his misery.

Pasting a smile on his face, he said, "Let's go, Abby."

She shook her head as she cuddled a kitten to her chest.

"We've got to go, or I'll be late."

She shook her head again, then gazed past him.

Leah said, "We'll come visit the kitties again, Abby. Don't forget there are kittens in the barn at Grossmammi's. They'd like you to pet them too."

James edged away as Leah held out her fingers. He said nothing when Abby set the kitten on the porch and stood, putting her hand in Leah's. He wished his daughter would reach out to him more often that way, but he needed to be grateful for each time Abby interacted with Leah. With her kindness, Leah was making a difference in Abby's life—and his own.

He waited until they were halfway across the field before he spoke the words he couldn't hold back any longer. "I didn't like the look Willard Eicher was giving you. Be careful with him, Leah."

"I know you're worried about Abby. You don't need to watch over me as if you're my Daed too." Her tone was light, so he knew she wasn't angry.

He was tempted to tell her he wasn't thinking like a father now. Nor did he say he'd read thoughts similar to his own in Seth's eyes while Willard was eyeing Leah.

The younger Eicher was interested in Leah, but whether his intentions were honorable or he was just looking for a good time with the new girl in town, James couldn't decide. He did know he didn't want Leah mixed up with the Eicher brothers. Quiet Seth and boastful Willard were alike in one way: They were focused on their own interests to the exclusion of everything and everyone else.

"I'm merely trying to be a friend." He struggled to ignore the bitter taste of the half-truth. Yes, he wanted to be her friend, but he also wanted more. When he found himself staring at her soft lips, he looked away before she could notice.

When they reached the truck, Abby pulled away and ran to it. She climbed in, then bounced out, holding a pamphlet. She offered it to Leah and gave her an expectant look.

"It's a brochure from a park," Leah said, her forehead wrinkling in confusion. "It looks lovely."

"It's Upper Falls Park," James answered. "Abby and I are heading over there next week. I think she'd like you to come with us." *I would too.* "How about it? Want to take a day off?"

Leah handed him the pamphlet and laughed. "A day off from what? I'm on vacation in Stony Brook."

"Is it a vacation when you help me by watching Abby?"

"That is something I love to do." She tapped the little girl on the nose.

"As well as doing the laundry, cleaning the house, and cooking?"

"I like to help, and I'm not doing everything by myself. I'm doing the tasks with Grossmammi, which is a special treat because I get to spend time with her."

"You've missed her since she moved to Indiana." He didn't make it a question. Why should he when he knew it was the truth?

"Very much. She was there when I needed her most. After my mother's death." Tears filled her eyes. "Now I'm here for her."

He started to speak sympathetic words, but halted. That could lead to a closer connection to her, and he needed to avoid that. Instead he heard himself say, "I've got research to do at Upper Falls Park. It's along Deer Lick Creek, a few miles from Richmond. That's the county seat for Wayne County. I plan to go next Wednesday because I don't have a class to teach or a meeting with my advisor. The weather's supposed to be nice, so I thought I'd take Abby along for a picnic. Why don't you join us?"

"To keep an eye on her while you do your research?"

He chuckled. "That's one reason, but I thought you might want to see more of the area while you're here."

As he spoke the words, he wanted to take them back. He wasn't sure how long Leah intended to remain in Stony Brook—she'd never said. Asking seemed impossible, because he was all too aware of the gulf that existed between her world and his. Friendship might provide a temporary bridge across it, as his need for a babysitter had brought them together. Whenever he was with her, he didn't want to think it was for the final time.

"Are there picnic grounds?" she asked as she met Abby's pleading gaze.

"There are some by the creek, I think." He opened the brochure and pointed at the map. "There they are. As you can see, the park is long and narrow and set between the creek and the road. However, there is an amazing collection of old-growth trees along with the undergrowth that thrives amidst them. Knowing how you like to learn about healing plants, you may find something to interest you." He knew he was laying it on a bit too thick, so he finished with, "Would you like to come with us?"

She hesitated. Then, looking again at Abby, she said, "Ja, I'll come and watch Abby, but only if I can bring a picnic lunch for us."

"I won't say no because my culinary skills extend no further than peanut butter-and-jelly sandwiches and fried eggs."

When her smile returned, he could hardly contain his happiness. Each of her smiles was like a gift, and he savored them.

"It's settled then. I'll make us lunch. No peanut butter-and-jelly sandwiches or egg sandwiches for you. Danki for asking me. Grossmammi mentioned in one of her letters that the park was a pretty place, and I'd like to see it." She smiled at Abby. "While your Daed looks at his trees, we'll look at leaves and flowers and everything upon the ground. Does that sound like fun?"

James held his breath, hoping his daughter would copy Leah's excited smile, but Abby only nodded.

These nods were more than he'd gotten out of her in the past year, so he should be grateful. He was, but he wanted to get back the chatty, giggling little girl she'd been. He was beginning to wonder if even Leah could reach through Abby's pain to return that happy child to him.

And what he'd do if what might be his last, best hope failed.

# 7

The day of their trip dawned sunny and with far less humidity than the previous evening. The heavy air had been washed away in the thunderstorms that had rolled across the low hills overnight. A few of the storms had been strong, but there hadn't been any damage in the Stony Brook area. A tornado might have touched down a few miles to the west, or it might have been extra-powerful winds that tore off the roofs of a gas station and a fast-food place. Nobody had been hurt, and the authorities were trying to confirm the cause of the damage, according to the newscaster on the radio playing in James's truck.

Leah settled herself on the front seat and pulled her sunglasses from her black purse. Setting them in place, she adjusted her seat belt before turning to check on Abby. The little girl, dressed in worn jeans and a pink T-shirt with a cat on the front, was paging through a picture book. She sat quietly, her feet rocking against the seat.

A pinch of despair taunted Leah. Of course Abby was sitting quietly. What would it take for the little girl to speak again?

*Lord, You know Abby's heart and the pain it contains. Please help us find the best way to reach into it so that pain can be eased. Show me how I can help.*

She'd prayed that every day, sometimes several times a day, since she'd learned that Abby didn't talk. God would answer. She must be patient. Knowing He loved each of His Kinder, she was sure He had a plan to help Abby and, through the Kind, to help James.

She wished he'd speak about his wife, but, until he mentioned

Connie and the accident again, Leah couldn't. *Is it only his family situation that weighs on him?* She'd seen how his gaze avoided hers when she spoke of her faith. Did he think she judged him because he was a Mennonite?

*No, that is silly.* If he thought that, he wouldn't have trusted her with his most precious treasure—his daughter.

James slid behind the wheel and reached for the key. His brows rose. "I didn't know Amish wore sunglasses."

"What would make you think we didn't?"

"Well, you eschew so many modern conveniences. I guess I figured sunglasses would be part of that."

"We like to live separate from the rest of the world so we can serve God with every thought and action of each day. Sunglasses don't connect me to the wider world. They just protect my eyes."

"I know there's a Bible verse dealing with being yoked unequally to nonbelievers."

"Second Corinthians 6:14. It says, 'Be ye not unequally yoked together with unbelievers: for what fellowship hath righteousness with unrighteousness, and what communion hath light with darkness?'" She looked at his strong profile.

His lips were tilted in a smile, which pleased her more than it should. If the rumors were true, and his wife had committed suicide, he needed every possible chance to smile.

"It's no burden," she added, "because Jesus promised to give us rest for our souls. He tells us to be yoked to Him, not to the world."

"It has to be difficult with the modern world pressing in around you."

"No one said doing as Jesus taught would be easy." She smiled to lessen the somberness of her words. "Isn't there a saying that anything too easy isn't worth having?"

He chuckled. "So that's why sunglasses aren't a problem."

"As long as we don't wear them for vain reasons. We aren't movie stars, after all."

That brought a heartier laugh. With a twist of the key, he started the truck and turned it to drive toward the road.

Leah waved to Ruth, who'd come out on the front porch. In amazement, she saw the older woman wasn't alone. Willard and Seth Eicher stood beside her. Seth was frowning, and Ruth looked anxious. Leah didn't see Willard's expression because he went into the house as the truck rolled past. She wanted to reassure her Grossmammi that nothing would come of her visiting the park with the Holdens.

She wondered if Ruth would believe her. The thought made her sad. Instead of growing closer to Grossmammi during this visit, she seemed to be finding more and more barriers between them.

---

Despite what James had told her and she'd seen on the map, Leah hadn't expected the park to run parallel with the main road for several miles. The entrance was an unmanned ticket booth made of logs. James drove into the parking area, which was barely wide enough for the truck to turn into a spot. A couple of cars were parked farther along the lot.

Leah lifted the picnic basket while James helped his daughter slip from her car seat. He settled a bright-blue baseball cap with a bright-red capital *M* on Abby's head. James wore an identical one, and Leah guessed it might be the logo of one of the colleges he was involved with. The *M* could refer to either Miami or Mennonite.

When he took the basket, she offered her hand to Abby. The little girl took it, but Leah noticed how her gaze darted back and forth, taking in the new sights. Was it a sign she was becoming more eager to become a part of the world around her?

James turned to shut the passenger door, then jumped out of the way when a shower of books cascaded onto the ground. Setting the basket on the curb, he began to gather up the thick books.

Leah lifted two and read the titles on the spines. One was *Trees of Central Indiana*. The other was another reference book about the flora of Wayne County. Though she would have liked to page through the latter, she handed both to James, who stacked the books on the floor so they wouldn't fall out again.

"These are samples of the books I use in my classes, as well a few I'm using for researching my thesis. I carry them around with me in case I have a spare moment." He paused and then asked in a careful tone, "Leah, are you interested in reading any of them?"

She looked at the titles on the truck's floor, then pointed to one in the middle of the pile. "I'd like to read that one."

"The Andrews book is a good basic overview of morphology. It's—"

"The study of plant structures and how the plants use them," Leah said with a grin.

Admiration widened his eyes, and she felt a mischievous pinch of delight at surprising him. He must have realized he was wearing his thoughts overtly, because he quickly said, "Sorry. I didn't expect you to know that."

"I live a plain life, but that doesn't mean I stopped learning when I left school," she said, making sure her voice didn't sound sharp. "I've seen references to this area of botany in other books. I'd like to read more about it, though I'm most interested in the diversity of plants and how we can use them."

"Then you'll want this one too." He handed her a thick red volume. "Wheeler and Davis is the go-to book for that."

Leah opened the book and scanned through it. As she read a few paragraphs, her trepidation that the text would be beyond what someone with an eighth-grade education could understand faded. The text was clear and straightforward.

"Danki," she said. "I'd like to read them, but if you need them for your thesis . . ."

"Those books are for my classes—the intro class and the more advanced one—and I can get other copies from the bookstore. Keep them for as long as you want. If you have any questions, I'd be glad to try to answer them." He chuckled. "I need to apologize again. Sometimes I get into the professor mode, and it's not easy to break out."

"It's okay." She handed the books back to him, then watched as he opened the front door and pushed them across to where she'd been sitting. "I'll probably have a lot of questions."

"Questions are good. They're how you learn. If you'd like to attend one of my classes, I'd be glad to have you there. It would give you an idea what the freshmen are studying."

The temptation to give him an enthusiastic yes was so strong she could taste the word. "Danki, but I shouldn't."

She could see he wanted to push the issue, but he nodded and gave her a faint smile.

"I understand," he said. "Perhaps it'd be better if you forget I suggested it."

"It would be for the best." She took Abby's hand again as he closed the doors and locked the truck.

Taking the basket, he didn't look at her. "If you change your mind, the invitation is open."

Leah decided the best answer was none.

The trail led along the creek. Leah wasn't surprised when James told her it was the swiftest current in the state. Water tumbled over stones, flying into the air and spraying everywhere before the drops fell and vanished.

"The elevation of the creek drops quickly," he explained, "which is why folks like to canoe or raft along it. The current actually runs as swiftly as the Whitewater River in Richmond. Despite the river's name, there isn't much real white water for adrenaline addicts, but it's fast enough for those who don't need their thrills to include being on the edge of death."

Leah chuckled. "You've got a way with words, James. Do you write like this in your thesis?"

"No way. That tome is as dry as desert dust."

"That doesn't sound *gut* when your topic is trees."

"Maybe I should change it to cacti." He rolled his eyes and gave a dramatic groan. "The thought of starting over is enough to make me curl up in a ball on the floor, sobbing. Not a pretty sight, I assure you."

"I'll take your word for it."

With a chuckle, he continued along the well-marked trail.

Unlike when she'd endured Seth's long-winded descriptions of his bees, Leah found what James said as he examined several trees fascinating. He was as obsessed with trees as Seth was with his hives, but James had a way of making his explanations interesting. She learned how the once numerous American beech trees had been chopped down by settlers and few survived. The trees that had been spared were over two hundred years old, outliving the more common white walnut trees nearby.

"When the settlers came to this part of the state," he said as he appraised the crown of the tree above him, "they made good use of the natural resources, including the trees, to build homes for themselves.

However, as more and more people settled here, the trees didn't have a chance to reseed and grow. The use of the land for farms devastated the trees even more."

She looked around them. "There are a lot of trees here."

"Some species were able to recover, while others have disappeared. I've been curious why certain types of trees bounced back and others didn't. That has been part of the scope of my thesis."

Abby wasn't listening to James. Instead she was collecting colored leaves along the path. Most were yellow oak leaves along with some orange and red maple leaves.

When Abby held up a bright red-and-green leaf with a tinge of gold, Leah said, "Lovely, Abby."

The little girl nodded, solemn as always.

"God created many beautiful things in our world, didn't He?" Leah kept going, knowing the Kind wouldn't answer. "It was a wunderbaar gift He has given to his Kinder, a world full of wonders. He shows us His love in letting us live in such a world."

She heard a soft grumble from James. Did he disagree with her words about God's love? Sorrow rushed through her. She couldn't imagine not having God in her life, knowing He was watching over her. Tears welled in her eyes as she realized losing his wife might have alienated James from his faith. If so, he'd lost more than she'd realized that tragic day.

---

James chided himself for reacting to what Leah had said to Abby. He didn't want to admit that he was envious of her faith, a faith he'd had before the deaths of those he loved had stripped it from him. He hadn't realized how much he missed being close to God until Leah had come into their lives.

As they emerged from beneath a canopy of trees, he heard Leah draw a quick breath at the view of a waterfall that dropped more than twenty feet into a pool. Trees and bushes clung to the sheer walls flanking it. Mist covered their leaves, causing them to glitter in the sunshine.

"It's pretty spectacular, isn't it?" James asked as he paused on a shelf of rock. It was smooth, as if someone had scraped and sanded it. Overlooking the pool, the ledge was far enough from the falls so the stone wasn't wet. "How about here for our picnic?"

Leah smiled and opened the basket he held. "This is perfect." Taking a blanket out of the basket, she shook it out and let it drift across the rock.

To one side, the waterfall created an ever-changing melody as the water cascaded along the rocks. A fine mist blew over them with each new breeze, but it wasn't enough to get them or the food damp. Instead it created rainbows in the air that lasted the duration of a single heartbeat before reappearing elsewhere.

They sat and watched as Abby spread out her collection of leaves. While James admired them, Leah took the food out of the basket. She'd wrapped sandwiches in waxed paper and placed other food in plastic containers or bags.

"The church spread is for Abby." She handed the packet to the little girl. "I've never met any Kind who doesn't like marshmallow crème and peanut butter." Pulling two more small plastic bags from the basket, she set them next to Abby. "Especially with sweet pickles and potato chips."

Abby took them, but no hint of a smile eased her somber face. She picked up the leaves and stacked them to one side, away from her dad.

Leah turned away, but not in time. James saw how she blinked back tears. Had she thought Abby would offer her leaves to him so he could discuss them with her? Like him, did she dare to believe each day could be the one when the little girl showed true emotion?

"I'm sorry," he said in a whisper as Abby opened her sandwich, the waxed paper crackling. "I know it's hard to get your hopes dashed."

She gave him a wobbly smile and handed him a wrapped sandwich.

They ate in silence, other than James telling her how much he enjoyed the thick slabs of roast beef on the bread he suspected she'd baked. He sipped the icy lemonade she'd brought in a thermos. The slices of apple pie were cut so they could eat them with their hands, and Leah drizzled honey on each piece before serving them. He wondered if he'd ever had anything so delicious.

He glanced at her lips and guessed they'd be even sweeter. He looked away. Why was he tormenting himself? When she said she wouldn't attend his classes, she'd made it clear she had no intentions of leaving her plain life.

Once they were done, Leah took Abby by the hand so she could clean the marshmallow and honey off her face with water from the pool. James offered to gather the remnants from their picnic.

As he did, James wondered why he hadn't taken the time to visit the park more often. Not only was it beautiful with the bushes displaying their fall colors, but birds sang overhead and a gentle breeze blew across the creek. It was a perfect day.

But the breeze and the birds had nothing to do with why the day was amazing. The day was special because of the company.

He put the last of the picnic items in the basket and watched as Leah and Abby played along the smooth rock. If it was a game, he couldn't figure out the rules. He suspected they were devising it as they went along.

Leah allowed Abby to set the pace. Somehow his daughter

seemed comfortable with Leah, who never pressed or tried to trick her into speaking. Abby clearly appreciated how Leah accepted her as she was.

Suddenly Leah cried out, the sound cutting through the air. James jumped to his feet and saw Abby stretched out on the stone. As he ran toward her, his daughter sat up, clutching her right leg. Blood stained her knee as tears ran down her face.

"Are you okay?" he cried.

"She's going to be fine." Leah knelt by his daughter. "Let's see what we can do to take away that ouch, okay, Abby?"

Continuing to soothe the girl, Leah used a wet napkin to wash the blood off what wasn't much more than a scrape. Abby's tears stopped. Leah opened a tiny container, dipped her finger into it and dabbed something shiny on the raw skin. Reaching into her apron pocket, she pulled out a bandage and put it over Abby's knee.

"Okay?" Leah asked.

Abby moved her knee, then nodded.

"*Gut.* Keep using your leg just as you always do, and it won't get stiff." She stood and rolled the paper wrapper from the bandage into the wet napkin. An easy toss dropped it into the picnic basket.

James stood when his daughter did and watched as she tested her right leg. Within moments, she began to skip around on the rock again.

"Astounding!" He picked up the basket.

"What?"

"How quickly she stopped crying! That must be a very special herb you put on her knee."

She smiled. "It was honey left over from lunch."

"Honey?"

"People have been using honey for centuries to heal small scrapes. You'd have to ask Seth why it helps. I'm sure he knows. I just know that it works." She reached into her pocket and pulled out a plastic bottle with an eyedropper in its lid. "I usually keep calendula for scrapes, but I happened to grab the honey first." She handed him the bottle. "Use a dropper of this and sterile water, mixing them half and half, on Abby's knee before she goes to bed tonight. Apply it in the morning every day for the next couple of days. Between the calendula and the honey, the scrape should heal soon."

He took the bottle and examined it. "What's the date on it?"

"The day I made the tincture. It's gut for about a year."

"As often as Abby skins her knees and elbows, I'll need this by the gallon."

She laughed, and the tight bands around his heart eased a notch. Enough to let its beat skitter in tempo with her laughter. When was the last time his heart had felt free? He couldn't remember. Not since the doctor had told them about Connie's devastating diagnosis shortly after Abby turned three.

"I'll see what I can do," she said, smiling.

Knowing he should say something to keep their lighthearted teasing going, he gazed into her sparkling eyes. The back of his fingers brushed her soft cheek, and her eyes grew wide. A sweet yearning flowed through him as he lowered his mouth toward hers at the same time he tilted her face toward his. She put up her hands, but yanked them back the moment her fingers touched him.

His good sense returned, and he kissed her cheek.

She gasped.

He grinned, hoping he could pull off acting nonchalant. "Don't look at me like that! I wanted to thank you for saving me from my own silliness."

"I don't know what you mean."

Wondering if he should be nominated for an Oscar for his

performance, he said, "For reminding me that every kid skins her knee now and then."

"Oh." She looked everywhere but at him. "You're welcome."

As she went to help Abby gather her leaves, James sighed. He was in trouble as far as Leah was concerned. That kiss had almost made his knees buckle, and it'd been on her cheek. The idea of sampling her pink lips made his head spin.

Yes, he was in deep trouble as far as Leah was concerned.

Heart-deep trouble.

# 8

A steady, chilly rain fell all day, a reminder that, though autumn hadn't officially started, winter lurked only a few pages away on the calendar. Leah was glad she'd decided to make a thick soup for supper. The cheese soup bubbled on the stove, the scents of potato, onion, celery, and plenty of black pepper filling the air.

It should warm her and Grossmammi inside and out. But she doubted it would reach the cold spot in her heart. She hadn't known that place existed until she'd seen James's smile coming nearer to her as he bent to kiss her yesterday. She was sure he'd planned to press his lips to hers.

Her reaction to keep him away had been automatic, but as her fingertips had jerked back from his firm muscles, she'd wondered why she was protesting. She'd been imagining him kissing her. She'd waited for his kiss. When it was a simple brush on her cheek and he said he felt grateful to her, iciness had sunk into her and refused to be dislodged.

The timer chimed and Leah opened the oven door to take out the casserole pan that held the spoon bread she'd prepared earlier. She was glad Ruth had an air-powered mixer because it would have been a laborious process to stir the cornmeal into the mixture of eggs and milk by hand.

"Everything smells *gut*," Ruth said as she came into the kitchen. She wore a well-starched Kapp on her hair, and her face was freshly scrubbed.

Both were sure signs, Leah had learned, that the older woman had enjoyed a nap before supper. While her Grossmammi hadn't been as sickly as she'd led Leah to believe, Ruth certainly moved at a much slower pace than she did in Leah's memories. Perhaps Leah should write her family and suggest that she stay in Stony Brook through the winter, because she didn't like the idea of Ruth living alone in the big house and having the responsibility of the chores as well as supervising the two boys who came to mow the grass and tend the animals.

Remaining in Indiana would, however, leave her Daed by himself on the farm in Pennsylvania. Her brother and sister and their families lived nearby, yet he'd be alone in the sprawling farmhouse. *If Daed would turn over the farm to Fred and move into the Dawdi Haus, it'd make things so much easier,* Leah thought. *Fred is eager to take over the farm and quit his job in construction, and his wife would take* gut *care of Daed.*

But her stubborn father refused to accept that the time had come for him to enjoy the fruits of long years of hard labor. Leah wasn't sure if her dad believed his son when Fred assured him that he could continue doing as much or as little work as he wanted on the farm.

Or maybe Leah's sister was right. Elsie had often said Daed had been a widower for too long, and he needed a loving wife to manage his life for him. A wife might point out that the time had come for him to take his place as patriarch of the family.

Had Ruth considered remarrying? Five years was a long time for an Amish widow to remain unwed. Ruth was energetic and enthusiastic. The way she laughed with her friends made them sound like a group of young girls on their way to a youth event.

Leah had to admit that staying to help Ruth wasn't the only reason she'd like to remain in Stony Brook. Whenever she thought of returning to Pennsylvania, she was ripped apart at the idea of never seeing Abby again.

*And James.* He constantly filled her thoughts.

His offer for her to attend one of his classes lurked at the edge of her mind, ready to tease her into visiting the college. A single trip would let her see what it was like to attend. It was a school for plain students, and though none of them would be Amish, she wouldn't feel like a complete outsider.

No, she couldn't do that. Attending a college class would be seen as a step away from the Leit.

She knew what she needed to do about James's invitation, but what was she going to do about her growing attraction to him? The moment by the falls when the world had vanished except for the two of them, her lips had been ready to welcome his.

She hadn't kissed anyone not related to her since she'd kissed one of the boys at her school on a dare from another scholar. She'd been in sixth grade. A couple of the young men had indicated they'd be happy to kiss her when they took her home from youth events, but she hadn't wanted to lead them on when she considered them friends.

Everything had changed when she'd gazed into James's eyes by the waterfall.

"It smells truly wunderbaar," Ruth said, her no-nonsense voice breaking into Leah's thoughts. "What is it?"

"Cheese and vegetable soup. A little bit of every leftover in the kitchen." Leah, relieved not to be enmeshed in the spinning swirl of her thoughts, spooned soup into two bowls and set them on the table. Freshly baked spoon bread and apple butter were waiting there, along with slices of the cold ham left over from their midday meal yesterday.

"I love cheese soup. You're spoiling me, Leah."

"Everyone deserves a little spoiling now and then." She pulled out her chair and sat.

When Ruth bowed her head for silent grace, Leah did the same. She was thankful for the food and the chance to spend this time with her Grossmammi. The memories they'd made when Leah was a child were now being overlaid by their time together as women. It was much the same, because Ruth had remained a loving presence in Leah's life, but now they were more like equals instead of a heartsick Kind in dire need of someone to fill in for her Mamm.

"It's as scrumptious as it smells," Ruth said after taking her first bite. "You must write out the recipe. I'd like to make it myself."

Though she knew pride was wrong, Leah couldn't help grinning. She never imagined Ruth asking her for a recipe.

"I'll do that," she replied as if Ruth asked every day.

"Your nose is a brighter red than earlier."

Leah nodded, taking care not to wrinkle her nose. She'd made that mistake earlier, and the sunburn she'd gotten yesterday sent pain across her face. "I didn't apply sunscreen as often as I should have when we went to the park. I put aloe on it a few hours ago. I should put more on it after we finish eating."

"Brew some tea."

"Tea?" She stared at Ruth, confused. "Why?"

"If you brew a dark tea and let it cool, you can dab it on the sunburn. The tannins in the tea will ease the pain and protect your skin. Not that it will keep your skin from peeling, but it'll make you more comfortable."

"I didn't know that." Leah lathered a slice of bread with apple butter and took a bite. Not a big one, because that would move her nose enough for another pulse of pain.

"This old dog still has a few tricks to teach a young pup like you." Ruth winked before ladling another spoonful of the thick soup into her bowl.

"I'm glad you do."

"So am I." She twirled her spoon in her soup before continuing. "Leah, it bothers me to see a *Maedel* like you unwed."

Leah's fingers froze with the slice of bread halfway to her mouth. Forcing her hand to lower, she set the bread beside her bowl. "Grossmammi, I'll wed when I meet the right man. Things happen in God's time."

"Giving God a little help never hurts." She set her spoon in her soup and leaned toward Leah. "I want to see you happy."

"I'm happy being here with you."

"I know. You like taking care of people. You've taken care of your Daed, and now you're taking care of me as well as the Englisch Kind. That shows me you would be happy taking care of a family of your own."

"That Englisch Kind's name is Abby."

"I know her name, and I know you're spending too much time with her and her Englisch Daed. How will you find a man to be your husband if you spend your time with a man you can't marry?"

It was difficult to keep her face from displaying her reaction to the question. Leah knew there was no future as man and wife for James and her. She liked him far more than she should, but she was realistic. However, to hear someone else say how impossible it was for her and James to be together threw a cloak of melancholy over her.

"I'm sure I'll meet someone I can marry," she said, knowing the older woman expected an answer.

"Maybe you've met that man already."

"It's possible. When I return to—"

"No, I mean here in Stony Brook." A broad smile brightened Ruth's face. "You and Seth would make a *gut* couple."

"We barely know each other."

"He knows enough about you to be interested in learning more. He talks about you a lot."

Leah wanted to retort that Seth's sole topic of conversation was taking care of his bees and hives. Saying that would upset Ruth, who seemed pleased at the idea of Leah marrying and remaining nearby. So instead of stating the truth, Leah changed the subject to other ways to heal sunburn with herbs.

As soon as they'd finished their supper and shared another silent prayer of thanks for the meal and the chance to be together, Leah set the kettle on the stove. She poured boiling water into a cup with a tea bag and let it steep for several minutes. When she was about to take the tea bag out, Ruth urged her to leave it for at least five more minutes.

"You want it strong," the older woman said. Going into the downstairs bathroom, she returned with a box of cotton balls. "Use these to dab on the tea once it's cool."

"Won't it turn my skin a different color?"

Ruth chuckled. "Your skin is already a different color! Whether your nose is red or brownish-red, what difference does it make?"

Leah laughed, then wished she hadn't when the top of her nose hurt. She hoped neither James nor Abby had gotten sunburned. Her heart bounced in anticipation of going into Stony Brook tomorrow to discover if their baseball caps had done a better job protecting them than her bonnet had her.

When Ruth walked across the kitchen to where two black bonnets hung on pegs, Leah asked, "Are you going out?"

"*Ja.*"

"It's cold out there."

"It's Thursday, Leah. You know I go out on Thursday evenings." She reached for her black bonnet. "There are snickerdoodles in the jar, and help yourself to the hot cocoa if you want." She gave a little shiver. "You're right, it's going to be chilly tonight. I fear winter is going to come earlier than usual this year because it seems like fall is over before it's started, ain't so?"

Leah didn't want to be distracted by a discussion of the weather.

She was bothered because her Grossmammi, who spoke candidly about every other subject—including Leah's love life, or lack of one—refused to say a single word about why she and her friends got together every Thursday evening.

"When will you be—" Leah began, but caught herself when she realized she was talking to an otherwise empty kitchen as the door closed.

For a moment she considered chasing after Ruth, but what was the point? Ruth Kauffman was a stubborn woman, and having decided she wasn't going to share what was going on, she wouldn't reveal a single word.

Sighing, Leah turned to the cup of tea. She almost poured it down the sink, but being spiteful wouldn't do any *gut* or change anything. And it definitely wouldn't make her nose feel better.

She cleaned the kitchen and washed the supper dishes as she waited for the tea to cool. Half of the soup remained in the pot, so she poured it into a glass container and put it in the refrigerator. She turned down the propane lamp hanging over the table before walking to the living room. She hadn't written Daed in a few days, so she'd use the time alone to send him an update on her visit.

*Does Daed have any idea what his Mamm is up to?* Leah couldn't ask, because she didn't want to upset him about Ruth's peculiar behavior.

The kitchen door rattled.

Leah whirled. *Was Grossmammi back?*

She stared as the door opened to reveal Naomi Byler.

Before she could stop herself, Leah asked, "What are you doing here tonight? Aren't you getting together with Grossmammi?"

"Oh, it's Thursday!" Naomi blushed from her double chins up to her scalp beneath her gray hair. "How could I have forgotten the day?"

"So the four of you are meeting at the Masts' house?"

"We better be." The older woman chuckled, but it sounded forced to Leah's ears. Without another word, she scurried out the door, and within seconds, the sound of buggy wheels could be heard.

*Am I being too sensitive, looking for a clue that would prove Grossmammi isn't being honest with me?*

Something was wrong. Leah was sure of that, but what could it be? Ruth wasn't being forthcoming, and Naomi was just as reticent. Someone else beside the four elderly women must know the truth, but who?

---

Leah drove the buggy into Stony Brook the following afternoon. Her first stop was the Maple Shade Bed and Breakfast.

Dorcas was delighted to see her, especially when Leah offered to dry the baking dishes that had been used to make food for the guests that morning. They were alone in the kitchen, one that didn't look all that different from the one at the Kauffman farm except for the electric lights and appliances.

Taking the towel, Leah began to dry a measuring cup. "Your Aenti is one of my Grossmammi's *gut* friends. Did they meet when my grandparents moved here?"

"I think they've been friends longer than that." Dorcas didn't seem surprised that Leah wanted to talk about their relatives. "From what Aenti Naomi has said, they've known each other most of their lives. Aenti Naomi spent a lot of time in Pennsylvania visiting her grandparents when she was a Kind, so they must have met then." She dimpled. "Now they've teamed up with the Mast twins, and the four of them are inseparable. Maybe it's because my Aenti is a widow as well, and Ida Mae and Vera Jean never married. It's as if they've started their own elders' social club for a second *Rumspringa*."

"Do you think that's what they're up to on Thursday evenings?" Leah explained her concern and shared Naomi's odd reaction the previous night when she realized it was Thursday and Ruth wasn't home. "A social club? Don't be silly."

"I could say the same to you." Dorcas's gentle smile took the sting out of her words. "Leah, you don't need to worry about your Grossmammi and her friends. I'm sure they're involved in nothing more outrageous than making a quilt for a fund-raiser. A quilt they want to be a surprise. They've done that before."

"But why would Grossmammi avoid answering me if that's what she's doing?"

Dorcas gave a shrug. "You know your Grossmammi is a prankster."

"Ja, I do." She couldn't help thinking about how she'd come to Stony Brook because Ruth had made it sound as if she needed Leah's help.

"I think she's having fun with your curiosity."

How she wanted to believe Dorcas!

When her friend began to talk about coming out to the farm to study cooking herbs, Leah went along with the change of subject. If Dorcas had known anything to alleviate Leah's concerns, she would have said so.

*There has to be an answer, but where am I going to find it?*

---

James stood as still as the furniture in the bed-and-breakfast's dining room. Leah's voice emerged from the kitchen. He heard her tone when she spoke with Dorcas, though he couldn't discern the words. Something was bothering her. Something important.

He didn't want to eavesdrop in spite of his dismay at the troubled sound of Leah's voice. He should have turned on his heel and departed the moment he realized he was listening to a conversation that might be private. Moving now meant the chance of him making a sound and alerting the two women that he was lurking in the dining room.

When he heard Leah say she should get going, he knew he couldn't be found standing there. He reached the front door and opened it as Leah and Dorcas emerged into the foyer.

"Hi." It sounded stupid, but he didn't know what else to say.

"I didn't expect to see you here," Leah said.

"More termites?" teased Dorcas.

He forced his shoulders to relax as he shut the door. "No, thank goodness. I stopped by to bring Myra some of her favorite takeout." He raised the bag.

"That's kind of you, James." Leah smiled.

"I can't begin to repay Myra for what she did for Abby and me, but this is a down payment. Her favorite restaurant is close to the university."

Dorcas held out her hand. "I can put it in the kitchen if you'd like."

"In the fridge, please," he replied. "That's four-way Cincinnati chili."

"I guessed by that amazing smell of chocolate and spices."

"I'm sure Myra won't miss a bite or two if you can't resist."

Laughing, Dorcas went through the dining room and into the kitchen. She closed it behind her, and silence fell like a smothering blanket.

"What's that?" asked Leah, saving him from having to find something to say.

"What's what?"

"Four-way Cincinnati chili."

*Ah, a safe topic.* "It's a unique type of chili. Not like Texas chili. It's made with all kinds of spices, including cinnamon, and it has cocoa in it."

"So it's sweet?"

"Sweeter than Texas chili, but it has a bit of a kick to it. Cincinnati chili served over spaghetti is called two-way. For three-way, you add cheese. Four-way has onions sprinkled on top. Some people put beans on it instead of onions, but with onions is the way Myra likes it."

"Is there a five-way?"

"Yes. It's served with spaghetti, cheese, onions and beans. But there's no six-way."

"Interesting."

"Looks like you got sunburned."

She touched her nose. "I did. Did Abby get sunburned too?"

"She's fine." *At least as far as a sunburn goes.* Meeting her gaze, he said, "I've got to tell you I heard you and Dorcas talking in the kitchen. I didn't hear what you were saying, but you sounded upset."

"It's nothing."

He frowned. "Leah, it's not like you not to tell the truth."

"That is the truth, James. There's nothing you or I can do. Grossmammi is keeping a secret from me." She sighed. "Secrets and misleading half-truths. That's not like her. Maybe I should insist she see a doctor to have a checkup."

"Are you worried about dementia?"

She shuddered, shaking her head. "Absolutely not. Her mind is as sharp as a teenager's, so I may be looking for trouble where there isn't any." She stepped around him and reached for the doorknob. "I'm glad you and Abby didn't get sunburned."

He put his hand on her arm, though he knew he shouldn't. He enjoyed the sensation that bounced from her to him, as he'd known it would. He should let her go, but his fingers savored her soft skin beneath them.

"You're worried about your grandmother, I can tell. Is there anything I can do to help?"

She shook her head again and drew her arm from beneath his fingers. Without another word, she went outside, leaving him more confused than ever.

# 9

After Leah had finished the last of the ironing on the following Tuesday morning, she folded the ironing board. She carried it into the laundry room and smiled as she shut it into the closet where it was kept along with the broom and mop. Of all the chores that needed to be done each week, the one she liked least was ironing. Laundry was on Monday and ironing was on Tuesday like clockwork at the Kauffman farm.

It helped that most of Ruth's dresses as well as her own were made of polyester or cotton blends. However, Ruth's black aprons weren't, and they came out of the washing machine looking like prunes. Shaking them out and hanging them on the clothesline didn't get rid of the wrinkles. Leah had to sprinkle them with water, store them in the refrigerator and then iron each one to get the fabric smooth again. Even their starched Kapps that could scorch were simpler to take care of than the black aprons.

Tonight, while writing home to her Daed, she'd ask him to have her sister or sister-in-law buy some black polyester and send it to Indiana. It wouldn't take long for Leah to sew a batch of new aprons for Ruth. The amount of time saved would be invaluable as they continued to can the vegetables being harvested from the garden.

The hours spent tending the garden—weeding and watering—were paying off. Each morning they picked ripe vegetables, and in the afternoon they canned them. The shelves in the cellar were becoming crowded with a colorful display of mason jars filled with different vegetables and fruit.

Each time James dropped off Abby so Leah could watch her and still help her Grossmammi, the little girl had to visit the pumpkins and see how much deeper an orange they'd become since the last time she was at the farm. Abby sat and stared at the fifteen pumpkins as if she expected them to ripen in front of her eyes. She was far more interested in them than the herbs Leah harvested from the smaller herb garden located next to the vegetable garden.

When Leah came into the kitchen this morning, the drying herbs hanging from the ceiling created a patchwork of aromas, changing as she passed from one type to the next. Ruth was scraping one of the carrots she'd pulled from the rows of the second planting. She dropped the cleaned carrot into a colander in the sink and flashed a smile at Leah.

"Done with the ironing?" the older woman asked.

"Ja, for this week."

Ruth chuckled at Leah's tone as she used the scraper to rhythmically remove long strips of dusty brown and reveal the bright orange carrot underneath. "Let me do the ironing next week. That way, you'll have time to collect more of the herbs I know you want to study."

"Most of the plants here are the same as those in Pennsylvania, but I like to discover where they grow."

"You haven't changed a bit since you were a little girl and followed me around when I collected herbs. So many questions! The more I answered, the more you asked, until you had questions I couldn't answer."

"Then I'd come indoors and pore over your books about herbal healing."

"Which led to more questions." Ruth chuckled as she reached for another carrot and bent over the sink to clean it. "You've taken to the utmost the principle that we Amish continue to learn through experience after we're done with our formal education. You keep cramming your head with more knowledge."

"I like learning."

Leah was relieved Ruth wasn't looking at her because she was afraid the truth might be visible. What would the older woman say if she knew Leah had begun to envy James his opportunity to study with teachers who could help him discover more and answer his questions—or at least point him in the direction to learn the answers himself? Or that James had invited her to attend one of his classes at the Mennonite college, and although she'd told him no, she remained tempted to accept his invitation. The idea of sitting in a room with others who shared her passion for studying plants was intoxicating.

Leah thought "intoxicating" was the perfect description, because she wasn't thinking clearly when she longed for the chance—just once—to experience a college botany course. She'd been born and raised plain. She would become a full member of the Leit once she was baptized. *Not once have I questioned that, but now . . .* She shoved the thoughts into the depths of her mind.

"Shall I begin making dinner?" Leah asked.

"Ja, but make something light for us," Ruth said with a smile. "We'll be putting together a sturdy meal for supper."

"Sturdy?" She'd never heard that word used to describe food.

"Ja. Men don't like flimsy food like sandwiches or salads."

"Men?" Leah asked.

Ruth acted as if she hadn't heard Leah's question as she went on. "Men want roasted meat and gravy and a variety of vegetables." She tapped a finger against her chin. "What would you say to lamb chops? I saw the grocery store was having a sale, and I know they're one of his favorites."

"Whose favorite?"

"Why, Seth's. I assumed you'd guessed who was joining us for supper, Leah." Wagging a finger at her granddaughter, she laughed.

"You're a wunderbaar cook. I know that, but it's time Seth knew it too. There will be five of us tonight." She counted on her fingers. "You and me and Seth and Willard and their Grossdawdi. It'll be a pleasant evening, and I'll make sure you and Seth have time alone without us butting in."

"I doubt Abby will want me to leave her alone with the rest of you. She doesn't know the Eichers well."

"Abby?" Ruth's brow wrinkled in a frown.

"Remember? I'm watching Abby tonight."

Ruth's frown deepened. "I don't know if you're helping James by babysitting his daughter. There's going to come a time when you'll need to focus on your own Kinder, and he'll have no one to keep an eye on Abby."

"Well, I'm not going to have any Kinder before supper tonight, and I told James that I'd keep Abby here until he picks her up."

Leah instantly regretted her words and her sharp tone. Ruth's face fell like a Kind's when a treat wasn't coming as promised. After Leah apologized, Ruth began to list the food they needed to cook and the other things they should do before the Eichers arrived, but Leah could tell she was upset.

Leah added one more thing to the list. She needed to find a way to convince Grossmammi to stop matchmaking without hurting the older woman's feelings.

---

The dinner was a mess right from the beginning. Not the food, which turned out fine, but everything else. Abby had been clingy, upset over something. Perry and Seth arrived at the specified time, but Willard wasn't with them. As they reached the kitchen door, he'd remembered something he had to do and left with no further explanation.

During the meal, Perry and Ruth had chatted. Their efforts to draw Seth into their conversation had been less than successful, and Leah found it easier to focus on helping Abby cut her meat.

Ruth must have gotten tired of being subtle because when they'd finished the main part of the meal, she said, "Let's wait a while before we have the delicious peach pie Leah made for us. It's a nice evening. You young people should go out on the porch and enjoy it while we oldsters clear the table."

"I'll be glad to help," said Leah.

At the same moment Seth urged, "Why don't you two relax and chat while we clear?"

"Nonsense." Ruth waved her hands as if the motion could push them out the door. "Go ahead and enjoy yourselves. Abby, would you like to help us? We could use someone to sample the pie."

The little girl shook her head and grasped Leah's hand.

"It's okay," Leah said. "I told Abby one of these evenings we'd count the stars as they come out." When Ruth opened her mouth to protest, Leah added, "Like you and I used to do."

Ruth's eyes narrowed. Leah hadn't intended to upset the older woman more. Instead she'd hoped her Grossmammi would remember how much a younger Leah had loved spending time with her.

"Go," said Perry with his warm smile, "and have a *gut* time." He winked at Abby. "You'll see lots of them on a clear night like this."

Knowing that saying anything further would only make the situation more uncomfortable, Leah collected sweaters for them and took Abby out on the front porch. She sat on a rocker, and the Kind crawled into her lap.

Seth followed them, shutting the door behind him as if he wanted to make sure what they said wasn't overheard. He leaned against the porch rail, the strain on his face visible in the faint light.

Looking at her, he said, "I want you to know I had nothing to do with this evening's matchmaking."

Before Leah could reply, Seth blushed as red as the western sky. He started to mumble an apology, but she stopped him.

"I know what you meant, and I'm not insulted." She glanced at the door.

Through it, she could see Ruth and Perry choosing seats in the living room. While they wouldn't be able to eavesdrop on her conversation with Seth—or lack of it—through the thick door, they were as close as they could be on the chance they might catch sight of her and Seth together.

"I'm glad," he replied.

"You're a nice man, Seth, but my home isn't here in Stony Brook."

He glanced at the little girl curled against her, and for a moment she thought he was going to make a comment about Abby. Instead he asked, "So you plan to return to Pennsylvania?"

"Ja. That's always been my plan."

His pale brows rose almost to his hairline. "I was told you were moving here to stay."

"Whoever told you that was mistaken."

"It was your Grossmammi, and I think she's hoping it would be true. She's become much more spirited since you arrived."

Leah took her time before she answered. Grossmammi wanted her to stay. That wasn't a surprise, but Ruth shouldn't be telling everyone Leah had made a decision when she hadn't.

"I'm sorry you got dragged into her matchmaking, Seth," she said as she shifted Abby in her arms. "I'll talk to—"

"No!" He lowered his voice, looking as startled as she was by his abrupt fervor. "Leah, you need to at least pretend to be interested in me. Otherwise, I suspect your *Grossmammi* will turn to Willard as a match for you. That would be a disaster."

"Willard?" She silenced the rest of her reaction. Though Seth apparently had as low an opinion of his brother as she did, she knew she must choose her words with care. She didn't want to say something that would upset Seth more.

"It's disturbing that she thinks we're interchangeable," he added.

Leah bit her lip. She hadn't thought Seth Eicher could be accused of *Hochmut*, but obviously he was distressed at the idea of being tossed aside and replaced by his brother.

Standing, she set Abby on the chair. She went to Seth and said in a near whisper, making sure her words didn't reach into the house, "I'm sorry for the matchmaking. *Grossmammi* fears I'll be an *alt* Maedel." The thought of being an old maid left a bitter taste on her tongue.

"Impossible, because you aren't old, Leah."

She appreciated Seth's reassurance when he was caught in the matchmaking web too. "I'm unwed, and *Grossmammi* doesn't intend for me to remain in that state. I don't want to get married just to be married. I want to fall in love first."

"It doesn't always work that way." His acrid tone shocked her. Pushing himself to his feet, he clasped his hands behind him and began to pace. "I used to believe as you do, but falling in love can break your heart faster than you can imagine if your family has ideas for your future. I learned when I fell in love with—" He clamped his lips closed and stared at her, his ears turning as red as the leaves on the maple trees in the backyard. "Forgive me, Leah. I didn't intend to say that."

"It's all right." She touched his arm, wanting to convey her sympathy. "Don't worry. I won't say anything to anyone else, and I'll play along with the matchmaking if it'll help you and the one you love."

"Danki, but it's too late." His voice was despondent.

"It's never too late to try and save a true love."

"Sometimes love isn't meant to be."

She shook her head. "No, I won't believe that. Love is too important not to fight for. You know that as well as I do. Maybe even better, because you fell in love before me."

Mumbling something under his breath, he marched off the front steps and around to the back door. Moments later she saw him, wearing his straw hat and striding across the field between the two farms.

Leah looked from him to the closed door leading to the living room where she could see their grandparents chatting. She whirled when she heard footsteps on the grass in front of the porch.

James stood at the bottom of the steps. His expression was lost in the twilight, but his shoulders were as taut and straight as a tree trunk.

How much of her conversation with Seth had he heard?

---

Taking a slow, deep breath, James knew he owed Leah another apology for eavesdropping on her again. He hadn't meant to, but neither she nor Seth had noticed his truck pulling in. Their raised voices had reached across the lawn. He couldn't *not* hear them talking about love.

Leah's voice echoed in his head. *Love is too important not to fight for. You know that as well as I do. Maybe even better, because you fell in love before me.*

*Leah and Seth.* He had to admit that he hadn't seen that coming, but it was a logical match, and it sounded as if they were in love. That meant the emotions James had thought he saw in her eyes were nothing but his own dreams reflected back at him.

He released a deep breath, but it didn't ease the pain clamping its claws around his heart. He was relieved when his voice sounded normal as he asked, "Why didn't you tell me you were having company tonight? I could have found someone else to watch Abby. Dorcas helped last week, and Myra pitched in while we were at the bed-and-breakfast. I'm sure she would have been willing to help tonight."

"I didn't know we were having company until the last minute. Grossmammi sprang it on me a few hours ago." She tried to grin, but failed. "You don't need to worry. There's always room at our table for Abby."

There was the slightest pause, so short he didn't know if he would have noticed except that she wouldn't meet his eyes. Was she upset because he'd discovered her talking about love with Seth? He recalled that Amish couples tried to keep their plans secret until they were ready to announce their engagement. Did she think he might blab about what he'd overheard?

"James, if you'd like," she went on, "you can come in and have pie with us too. Or would you like supper? I can assure you there's enough food left over for an Amish wedding."

"I don't want to intrude." *Or hear you say anything more about Amish weddings.*

"You wouldn't be." She put her hand on his arm, and everything vanished from his head as he was suffused with the warmth radiating out from beneath her fingertips. He was overcome with a desire to kiss her. "Friends are welcome at our table."

What an idiot he'd been! Why would he think she thought of him as someone more than a friend? She was Amish, and she would never envision him as a possible suitor. When he'd been ready to kiss her in the park, he was sure he'd seen longing in her eyes. A longing that echoed his own to discover if the spark between them could become a flame.

He'd been wrong. "No thanks," he said as he motioned for Abby to join him. "Leah, I didn't mean to listen in again. Until I got close to the porch, I didn't realize you and Seth were having a private conversation."

"It's okay." She lifted her hand away.

"It seems things are working out for the best." He wondered if she had any idea how difficult it was for him to speak those trite words.

"It would seem so."

For once, he couldn't read her face. Was she being honest, or was she talking in clichés as he was to hide the truth of her feelings? She must be eager to marry Seth Eicher to talk of being in love after knowing him such a short time.

He frowned. *Maybe Leah and Seth were acquainted before she came to Stony Brook. That would make more sense.*

*No,* he argued with himself as he took Abby by the hand and led her to his truck and settled her in her seat. Nothing made sense. Nothing had in far too long. After he'd endured a year of mourning Connie, Leah had been the first woman who'd scaled the mountain of his pain to reach him. Had she even been trying? His attraction to her and how she'd opened her heart to Abby had misled him.

He had been as wrong about Leah as he had been about Connie. For a short time over the last couple of weeks or so while he'd lost himself in dreams of being with Leah, getting to know her better and discovering if she was as wonderful as she seemed, he'd set aside his guilt over his wife's death. He'd come alive again, dared to think of the future again, allowed his heart to begin to heal.

He wasn't sure he'd be able to ease his guilt again. Was it really possible his wife had become so desperate to escape her pain that she'd decided to kill herself even if doing so endangered their daughter? The battered car had been dented with white paint on the driver's side, revealing that the vehicle had bounced off a nearby plank fence before careening into a tree. Why hadn't Connie been honest with him? He could have helped.

He had to believe that. Instead, his wife had acted as if she were prepared for the surgery and chemo to come. He'd never doubted her assertion that she was determined to keep the cancer from killing her, but he hadn't guessed how she planned to ensure it. And he still wasn't sure he could believe it. Conflicting emotions warred within him. One day he accepted it. The next day he was certain it wasn't true.

Regardless, his guilt had resurrected itself. He wondered if he'd ever escape it now. He couldn't be sure, but he was sure he'd be a complete fool to risk his heart again.

*Never again*, he vowed, as he started the truck and drove off into the thickening darkness. *Never.*

# 10

"James? James, did you hear what I said?"

"No." James sat straighter and looked across the desk in front of him.

Neil Judd, PhD, was James's advisor on his doctoral thesis. The man looked less like a college professor and more like a pro wrestler. His bald head shone in the harsh light from the office lighting, and his face appeared to have been carved out of stone by an incompetent sculptor. Despite his thick neck, shoulders, arms, and fingers, he was skilled at slicing plants to create incredible slides to help his students appreciate the beautiful complexity of growing things.

His voice, as impossible to ignore as a fire siren in the middle of the night, could cut through a laboratory filled with undergraduate conversation. Even when it was the two of them, Neil spoke at the level of a sonic boom. Yet somehow James had become so lost in his thoughts that he'd failed to hear what Neil was saying.

"At least you're honest." Neil grimaced as he leaned back in his chair and clasped his hands behind his head.

James wasn't fooled by his advisor's apparent nonchalance. The awards and framed covers of academic magazines on the wall of the office that was as large as the kitchen at the Kauffman farm were an indication that Neil took his studies—and his students' studies—seriously.

"We've worked together too long," James said to his mentor, "for me to try to pull the wool over your eyes."

"You need to pull the wool out of your ears." Neil frowned as

James started to apologize again. "You've got something on your mind. Should we reschedule?"

James considered demurring, but he knew continuing their discussion now would be a waste of time. His *and* Neil's.

His advisor was right. James had something else on his mind. Some*one* else. Two someone elses.

*What are Leah and Abby doing now? Has Leah succeeded in her determination to reach past Abby's silence? How much longer will Leah be willing to watch her before wedding plans require all her attention?*

"How about next Friday morning?" James asked. "Around ten."

"Thursday afternoons—later in the afternoon—would be better for me. I can't do Tuesdays. They're pretty much consumed with department business." He gave James a genuine smile. "And Fridays will become a problem starting at the beginning of November, so I was going to talk to you about changing our regular meeting time anyhow. Is it going to be a problem for you?"

"It shouldn't be. I'll just need to get a babysitter for Abby." He'd have to ask Leah if she could take Abby on Thursdays. He had office hours for his own students on Thursday mornings, so that would make for full days.

"Good idea. Our discussions would bore a kid."

James nodded, knowing Neil was trying to be nice. James had made the mistake of bringing his daughter to a meeting with Neil once. It had been less than a month after Connie's death. He'd brought Abby with him because he'd been horrified to hear that, after his session the previous week with Neil, Abby had spent the three hours he'd been gone weeping inconsolably.

Had his daughter believed he had left her for good as her mother had? He couldn't be certain, but he'd held Abby that night until she fell asleep. When the next week rolled around, she had gone with him to the university—and he and Neil had gotten less done than they had today. At that point James had decided to take the rest of that semester off.

Not for the first time did he wonder if he was being fair to his daughter. He could have put his PhD thesis on hiatus for a full year or more. Everyone at the university had had sympathy for his loss and had been agreeable with whatever he decided. He hadn't wanted to wait, though. Connie had been the one who'd urged him to get his doctorate, and he felt an obligation to finish it in her honor once he could make his mind work enough to study.

But was he putting his studies before his child—or did she feel that he was? He hadn't guessed how difficult it was to be a solo parent to a traumatized little girl.

Standing up, James said, "I'll give you a call to confirm Thursday, okay?"

"Okay, and make sure you bring your A game with you, James."

"Got it."

Grabbing his coat off the rack by the door, James folded it over his arm as he walked along the deserted hall. Muffled voices came through the closed doors on either side of the corridor.

He paused when he reached the exit and grimaced at the rain. At least it wasn't a cold rain because the weather had warmed over the last few days. He appreciated the irony that, at the very moment his heart froze, nice fall temperatures had returned.

Ducking his head, he hurried to his truck and climbed inside. He reached to put the key in, then paused. His next stop would be the Kauffman farm. His efforts to find someone else to watch Abby had been futile, so he'd taken her back to Leah.

She'd welcomed his daughter as if Abby were her own. She'd acted kind to him. Was that what she wanted? To act as if the other night when he chanced to hear her speaking about love with Seth hadn't happened? He should be glad she hadn't slammed the door in his face or told him in no uncertain terms never to darken the Kauffman's threshold again.

She had been gracious, and now it was his turn to be grateful.

He leaned his head against the steering wheel. Years ago, before his best friend and his wife died, he would have reached out to God. Now . . .

*God holds Abby in His hands, and He'll bring her healing and peace when He knows the time is right. He's there for us every minute of our lives, not only in our times of need. We're never alone.* He heard Leah's words again in his mind and heart.

*Is she right?*

Without raising his head, he tried to pray. The words wouldn't come, no matter how hard he tried. He began to realize how much he'd lost along with Connie on the day Abby had lost her voice.

---

Abby stood by the door and stared out at the rain. She didn't need to speak a single word to reveal what was in her heart. The little girl had wanted to work in the garden this afternoon so she could check how much larger the pumpkins were.

Leah considered finding an umbrella so she could escort the Kind out to the garden. Ruth would think her mad to do such a thing, but she had an appointment at the eye doctor this afternoon and wouldn't be back until after James came for his daughter.

Her pulse quickened, because she was eager for the chance to be with James again. She'd tried to make her heart see reason since the uncomfortable conversation on the front porch. She'd failed. The idea of being with him added joy to her day. If only he'd been raised Old Order Mennonite instead of in his progressive church . . .

She was being unrealistic. Though the Amish had originated among the Mennonites, the gap between them now was vast. There was no "if only," just the reality of the different paths God had set them upon.

Leah pushed aside her bothersome thoughts when the little girl sneezed for the third time in as many minutes. It might not be the onset of a cold, but Leah wasn't going to take the chance of taking Abby out to the garden. Wet feet could bring a cold on faster and make it worse.

"Do you want to help me finish making cookies?" Leah asked, going to the refrigerator and taking out the dough she had set aside to chill a few hours ago.

Abby shook her head, staring at the rain. Did she think if she glared at it long enough the rain would go away?

"I could use your help."

With a sigh worthy of a martyr, Abby turned from the door and shuffled across the kitchen to the table where Leah was smoothing out the dough with a rolling pin.

"I used to make these sugar cookies with Grossmammi."

Abby glanced at her and then looked away.

Leah scooped up the dough and put it into the bowl. Stretching the plastic wrap over it, she set the bowl back into the fridge. The cookie dough could sit a bit longer. Abby needed her attention now.

"I have an idea for something fun we can do," Leah said as she washed the scattered flour off the table. "Let's make a mobile from pretty leaves."

The little girl looked up, intrigued.

"You must let me go outside and collect the leaves. I've got boots."

Abby ran to her backpack and opened it. She pulled out a manila envelope. Turning it upside down, she sent more than a dozen leaves tumbling onto the table. She chose one and arched her brows.

It must have been one of the leaves the little girl collected when they went to the park with James, because it had lost most of its color and faded to a dull brown. Abby acted as if it were the most beautiful thing in the world.

"How about if I get a couple of leaves from here on the farm for you to add to your mobile?" Leah asked. "That way you'll have some from the park and some from here. Do you like that idea?"

Abby nodded.

"While I do that, you can go into the living room and get a spool of thread from Grossmammi's sewing box. Be careful of the needles and pins, okay?"

The little girl rushed into the other room.

Leah went outside and gathered a handful of brilliant red maple leaves. She was glad her kerchief was on her head instead of her Kapp, because the organdy would have wilted beneath the raindrops.

She wasn't surprised to see that Abby had brought red and bright green thread from the sewing box. The little girl wouldn't have been contented with the simple white thread Leah had envisioned.

Giving the Kind blunt-end scissors, Leah showed Abby the variety of lengths of thread they'd need and put the little girl to work cutting them.

Leah found a block of beeswax in a cupboard in the laundry room. Filling the bottom section of a double boiler with water, she fit the two pots together. She put the wax in the top and turned on the gas burner. Using the old spoon Grossmammi kept for melting wax to seal jam jars, she stirred the wax so it didn't scorch.

It didn't take long to melt the block into a clear liquid. Setting the heat so the wax wouldn't harden again, she went to the table where Abby waited.

"You select the leaves, and I'll dip them." Leah tore off a piece of aluminum foil and spread it out on the table for the freshly waxed leaves. Leah gave the little girl a stern frown as she said, "You must promise me you'll stay away from the pot. Today you're going to learn how to wax these leaves, but you can't do this on your own until you're grown up. Okay?"

Abby nodded, as serious as if she was about to embark on open-heart surgery.

"Which one first?"

Abby selected a maple leaf. It was a kaleidoscope of colors, with red and gold vying for dominance.

Leah gripped the stem between her thumb and index finger. With care she lowered the leaf into the liquid wax. Lifting it, she let the extra wax drip into the pot. She repeated the motion two more times to make sure the wax would be smooth on the leaf, but not so heavy that the colors wouldn't show through.

Setting the leaf on the foil, she motioned for Abby to stay back until the wax had a chance to cool.

The little girl looked at the leaf and frowned.

"I know it looks cloudy now," Leah said, "but once the wax hardens, the colors will reappear. Which one next?"

Leah kept up a steady chatter while she dipped the leaves. Once she'd done half a dozen, she gave the little girl a glass of lemonade to distract her long enough for Leah to clean the waxy mess. The leaves were cooled by the time Abby was finished, so Leah helped Abby tie the threads to the stems of the leaves. Taking one of the seals used for closing mason jars, Leah punched holes around it and, with a needle, drew each thread through the rubber. She tied them off, added a trio of other threads for hanging the mobile, and then held it up.

Abby clapped her hands in delight as the leaves fluttered against one another on the simple mobile when Leah hung it from a towel pole over the sink.

"It's pretty, ain't so?" Leah asked.

The door opened as if in reply to her question. About to greet Ruth, Leah was astonished to see James enter instead. She hadn't expected him so soon. She refrained from giving into the instinct to smooth loose strands under her kerchief.

Abby jumped off her chair and ran to grab his hand. James didn't resist when she tugged him over to the sink. She pointed at the mobile. He looked from it to Leah.

"We made it from leaves in the yard and ones Abby collected at the park," she explained. "Abby picked out which leaves to use."

"You did?" He squatted next to his daughter. "It's pretty. Almost as pretty as you are, sweetheart."

Turning to the table, Abby grabbed a leaf they hadn't used. Offering it to her father, Abby smiled.

She actually *smiled*.

Leah swallowed her gasp of amazement and looked over the little girl's head to see tears welling up in James's eyes. Her own eyes burned with tears of joy. She pressed at the inner corners of her eyes to keep them from falling.

James turned his face away from his daughter. Like Leah, he knew that if Abby saw them crying, she might not understand why. That could upset her and steal her precious smile.

"Thank God," he murmured as Abby ran to the table to get more samples of the waxed leaves. Walking around the table to where Leah stood, he stopped in front of her. "You've brought about a miracle here today."

She breathed in the scent of him, as earthy as the drying herbs overhead. It was a combination of his woodsy aftershave, soap, and book dust from his hours of study. She couldn't imagine anything more enticing. It took all her willpower to keep from brushing aside the damp hair on his brow.

"If there was a miracle today, it was because of God," she whispered, not trusting her voice to speak louder. "All that is *gut* comes from Him."

"This goodness came from you, Leah."

"I'm just His conduit to reach into Abby's heart."

"Not only hers. You've touched many lives since you came to Stony Brook." His gaze caught hers, holding her as surely as if he'd wrapped his arms around her. "I've heard God works in mysterious ways, but there's nothing mysterious about how you've persevered when others have given up."

"You never have."

"I've considered it more often than I care to admit."

"What we think we *might* do is far less important than what we actually do."

Leah said nothing more as Abby rushed back to them and offered James a bouquet of the waxed leaves.

He knelt on the floor and examined each one as if it were a revelation. Abby kept smiling.

---

James struggled to speak past the lump in his throat as he finished helping Abby put on her coat. His daughter's eyes gleamed in a way he hadn't seen in the past year. And her smile—was it the answer to his prayer?

No, Leah was. She'd been ready to help before he had reached out in prayer. She would say God had put her in his life, and he wanted to share the faith she possessed. But he couldn't, not when other prayers had gone unheard and his wife and his best friend had died. His efforts to regain his faith—putting aside his studies for two years to try to ease the loss of Brian's death by helping the ones his best friend had tried to help—had been futile.

His uncertainty wouldn't stand in the way of his gratitude today.

"Thank you," he said, hoping Leah realized his words weren't aimed solely at his daughter, who handed him the mobile so she could pull on her backpack. "This is wonderful." He chuckled and winked at Leah, though the motion threatened to send happy tears down his cheeks. "Or maybe I should say it's wunderbaar."

"Any way you say it, it's the truth," Leah replied. "Abby worked so hard and did such a great job with preserving the leaves, ain't so?"

"She did." He bent and held out his arms to his daughter.

Abby grinned, throwing one arm around him and the other around Leah.

Knowing he was playing with fire, but not caring for the moment, he put his arms around his daughter and the woman who had broken through the pain he and Abby shared. He drew them close, savoring the sweet scents of their hair. Abby's smelled like bubble gum, but Leah's was more sophisticated—a blend of citrus and flowers. The combination was as enticing as she was.

When Leah's arms curved around him and Abby, he almost forgot to breathe as he relished the sensation of holding them close.

No, he wouldn't lie to himself. He was thrilled to hold Leah. She seemed to fit perfectly against him.

He smiled and was rewarded when Leah and Abby both smiled at him. The glorious moment lasted for only the time it took his heart to beat once before the door opened.

As he moved out of the way, releasing Leah and his daughter, Ruth

Kauffman came in. Her words of greeting died on her lips when she saw James standing beside her granddaughter. When Leah urged Abby to show Grossmammi the mobile they'd made, Ruth's eyes continued to return to him.

There was no mistaking her message. She wanted him far away from her granddaughter.

He knew she was right. There wasn't any place in Leah's life for him, but how could he walk away? The answer stole every bit of joy from him, because if he cared for her at all—and he did—he must not put her into the position of choosing between him and her faith.

# 11

"Danki for offering me a ride home," Leah said, hoping her words would shoo away the silence in the buggy where she sat with Seth.

It contrasted with the cacophony of voices that had left her ears ringing at the youth event. Instead of the group singing on a church Sunday, they'd had a taffy pull. As fast as the candy could be made on the stove, there were couples eager to spend time flirting while they stretched the candy over and over until it was smooth and cool enough to cut into small pieces.

Not many of the participants had bothered to try the candy. They were more interested in chatting and listening to the radio someone had smuggled into the house. It'd been turned up high. Leah was grateful there had been fresh, sweet cider to ease her throat after having to shout to be heard.

The evening with laughter and jokes and debates about favorite sports teams had been the opposite of the quiet, reverent service that morning. Both had lasted about the same amount of time: three hours. While the church service had lifted her spirits, leaving her feeling as if her soul had expanded, the taffy pull left her exhausted as she tried to remember the names of so many strangers.

"I drive right by your Grossmammi's farm on the way home," Seth said in response to her comment, not taking his eyes off the horse in front of them. That was smart, because the twilight had vanished into a thick fog rising off the harvested fields on either side of the road. "It would have been foolish for someone else to travel a mile or more out of their way to bring you home."

"You're right."

She waited for him to answer, but he didn't.

Pulling her black cape around her, Leah let a soundless sigh drift past her lips. She gazed out into the fog that seemed to grow thicker and chillier by the second.

Not as chilly as the space between her and Seth.

When Ruth had urged her to attend a youth event in the next district, Leah had wanted to demur. She'd attended enough of such gatherings in Lancaster County. Singings and softball games and taffy pulls and cookie making and frolics to clean an elderly person's home or help with farm chores. She'd gone to them until the last year when it seemed as if most of those attending were a lot younger. Many people her age had paired off and were married. Some had Kinder already.

Ruth had been insistent. Leah shouldn't spend every daylight hour working in the house and helping her Grossmammi or watching someone else's Kind.

"You're a young woman," Ruth had stated in a tone that brooked no argument. "A young woman should have fun with other young people."

Despite that, Leah had tried to postpone attending any youth events in Stony Brook. Ruth had given in until today, when she was firm about Leah going with the express order to have fun. She even drove Leah to the event and dropped her off.

Leah was no closer to figuring out which girl was the one Seth loved. He'd spent the whole evening with male friends until he asked if she wanted a ride home. Overall she'd had a *gut* time, but there had seemed to be something missing.

Someone.

Nobody at the party had been as interesting as James when he spoke about plants and trees. She'd found herself offering polite smiles instead of the laughs that burst from her when she was with him. She'd discovered that she felt most herself when she was with James.

"How are the bees settling in?" Leah asked, hoping to restart their stalled conversation and at the same time stop thinking about a man she must never consider more than a friend.

"Fine. I moved them outside and took off the tarp." Enthusiasm filled his voice.

"They didn't fly away?" she asked.

"No. Of course, they're getting ready for winter, and they won't be active until it's warm again. Because the hive is new, they'll begin filling their hive with honey in the spring. They should make enough over the summer to take care of themselves next winter. The year after, I'll be able to start harvesting honey."

"How did you learn so much about bees?"

"Before your grandparents bought their farm, the old man who lived there was a beekeeper. He saw how interested I was, so he taught me everything he knew about them." He gave her one of his rare smiles. "That was a lot."

"Like Grossmammi teaching me about herbs."

"Ja. At the time, I thought about learning all I could so I could someday have hives of my own. Now I realize how important it is that the knowledge gets passed down from one generation to another."

"I agree. That's why I started teaching others about herbs back home in Pennsylvania. I've been asked to do the same here, but I haven't had the time yet. However, the more who know, the less likely the lore will be lost."

"Perhaps I should start finding apprentices too. My brother doesn't have any interest in learning about bees."

"What is Willard interested in?"

"Besides you?"

Leah gasped. "I wasn't fishing for compliments, Seth."

He let his elbows rest on his knees. "I shouldn't have said that, Leah. Embarrassing you wasn't my intention, but it seems like you're all he talks about. He hasn't made any secret of being interested in you. He wants to know when you have Abby staying with you."

"Why?"

"I guess because he's hoping to have a chance to spend time alone with you." Seth sighed. "Like I told you, Willard has changed over the past year. He's not always skipping church. It seems he's trying to be a better man. At least that's what Grossdawdi believes."

"Do you believe it too?"

For the first time, his gaze met hers. "I want to believe it, Leah, because he seems serious this time. He sold his car to a friend, a big, old white Cadillac that he loved even though he had to tinker with it to keep it going. But then I smell alcohol on him, and I know he's been drinking with his Englisch friends again, and I question if he's ready to make the commitment to the Amish life."

"You said he's been taking baptismal classes."

"He was. Now he's not there half the time for the classes on Wednesdays and Sunday mornings." He frowned. "I'm tired of having to devise excuses for the bishop and the deacon about why Willard isn't with me."

"So you're taking the classes too? When do you plan to be baptized?"

"Next month." He flushed, the tips of his ears looking in the buggy lights as if they'd been scalded. "Maybe then you would consider walking out with me."

Leah shook her head. "Seth, I don't know who you're in love with, but it's not me. So why are you asking to walk out with me?"

"Grossdawdi says you'd make me a *gut* wife, and I should look at what a fine woman your Grossmammi is. You and I get along okay, ain't so?"

She made quotation marks in the air. "Is 'getting along' enough for you?"

"I don't know."

Reaching out, she put her hand on his. She didn't feel the strong pulse she did when she touched James. Oh, how much simpler it would be if she felt a connection with Seth instead!

"We're friends, Seth," she said. She guessed he was trying not to push aside her hand. *Why? Because he doesn't want me to stop touching him or because holding hands feels as strange to him as it does to me?*

"Ja." His voice was as stiff as he was.

"As your friend, I want you to be happy. My Grossmammi and your Grossdawdi had marriages based on love and joy. They believe you and I could have the same, but we know that's not true. Your heart belongs to someone else."

Again he looked at her. "Are you in love with another, Leah?"

It wasn't a lie when she said, "I don't know, but what I do know is that I want to be wed to someone who is more than a friend. He needs to be my best friend. Exactly as the woman you love could be yours if you forget about what your Grossdawdi wants and think about what you want."

"What Grossdawdi wants is more important to me than what I want." A note of finality filled his voice.

Leah had no answer, though she had a lot of questions. She admired Seth's devotion to his family, but why would he agree to his Grossdawdi's plan when a less-than-happy marriage would also have an impact on the older man? *Marrying someone else would hurt the woman he loved, ain't so? Unless it's an unrequited love, or the woman isn't one he should consider marrying because she's already married or isn't Amish.*

Sorrow rushed through her. Had Seth fallen in love with an Englisch woman? Once he was baptized, marrying her would mean him being put under the *Bann*. As devoted as he was to his family, she knew he wouldn't want to be separated from the Leit and every plain person he knew. Seth had made his choice.

Now it was her turn. Could she set aside her dreams of true love in order to make someone else happy by marrying Seth and staying in Stony Brook? The answer should be simple, but when that someone else was her Grossmammi, it was anything but.

---

James yawned as he turned his truck onto the road leading toward the Kauffman farm. He liked interacting with his students, but Thursdays when he had office hours and then had to drive to Ohio to meet with his advisor left him feeling sapped.

He needed to talk to his department head and change his office hours to another day. Each student had unique needs, and he didn't want to shortchange them by not giving them a chance to get his help. He wanted his students to succeed, so he spent as much time as necessary answering their questions or pointing them in the right direction to discover what they needed to know. As the students had become more familiar with him now that he was in his fourth semester teaching at Eastern Indiana Mennonite College, they seemed eager to get his opinion on a variety of subjects, including financial aid, future job prospects, and their relationships with either roommates or girlfriends and boyfriends.

He wanted to tell them that he was the last person on campus they should come to for advice on love. He'd made a mess of everything again. After overhearing Leah talking to Seth, he'd known for sure that she was off-limits to him. It hadn't made a difference when his joy at Abby's first smile in a year banished his common sense. Letting Ruth discover him with his arm around Leah had been a big mistake.

Or so he assumed. Leah had been just polite when he dropped Abby off that morning. She refused to meet his eyes, and it seemed that she couldn't wait to shoo him out the door.

Driving toward the house, James warned himself to play it cool. His life was a mess, and Leah deserved better than getting sucked into it.

His plan lasted long enough for him to get out of his truck, walk to the house, and open the kitchen door. Any attempt at appearing self-controlled vanished the moment Abby ran to him and flung her arms around him. He fought not to react with outward surprise, but his heart leaped about in his chest like tree branches in a tornado. First Abby had smiled, and now she acted happy to see him. She was again becoming the sweet daughter he'd feared was as lost as his late wife. Whether the change was the result of a single event or the combination of the time she'd spent with Leah, he couldn't guess.

He raised his eyes, and his gaze locked with Leah's. Abby's reaction to his arrival had stripped away the chilly façade she'd exhibited that morning, revealing that her delight matched his own. Again his heart exulted, and he knew he'd never again question whether Leah cared about him and his daughter. Leah might not feel the same attraction that drew him to her, but she wanted the best for him and Abby.

With a soft cry Leah broke the connection between them and whirled to face the stove. Wisps of smoke rose from a cast-iron pan along with the odor of hot oil.

"What are you frying?" he asked as he came to his feet, keeping his hand on Abby's shoulder. He'd sampled Leah's delicious fried chicken one noon when he'd brought Abby to the house. He doubted Leah was making that at this hour because he'd learned that the Amish who lived on farms had their large meal at midday.

"Fried mush," she replied with a smile.

His nose wrinkled. "Does it taste better than it sounds?"

"It does." Her grin broadened, and he knew he'd eat anything if she served it with her scintillating smile. "Abby and I were about to eat. Abby, get a cup and silverware for your Daed."

As his daughter rushed to obey, he nodded at Leah's request for him to sit at the table. He pulled out a chair at the spot where Abby put a coffee cup and a spoon along with a fork and knife. Thanking his daughter, he hid his surprise that she knew the right way to arrange the silverware. Leah was teaching her all sorts of things in addition to what was in the textbooks piled at one end of the counter.

Leah set a plate in front of him, and he gawked at it. He'd thought anything named mush would be served in a bowl like oatmeal. Instead, on the plate was a stack of what appeared to be pan-fried cornmeal pancakes.

Laughing, she filled his cup with fragrant coffee before she sat facing him. She bowed her head over her folded hands. Abby copied the motion, and James did the same. He remembered the Amish way was to pray in silent communion with the others at the table.

He had no idea what Leah or Abby prayed, but his was a simple, *Thank you, Lord. Thank you. Thank you.* It wasn't much of a prayer, but he was rusty when it came to talking to God. He was sure the Lord would understand the depths of his gratitude.

Leah raised her head and pushed a bottle of maple syrup toward him. "Put this on your fried mush. I like it best with syrup dripping down the sides."

He poured golden syrup on the mush, then did the same for Abby. As he handed the bottle to Leah, he asked, "Where's your grandmother tonight?"

"It's Thursday. She goes out on Thursday evenings."

"Every Thursday evening?"

"Ja, no matter the weather." She closed the top of the bottle after putting syrup on her mush.

James took a cautious bite of the food in front of him. His eyes widened when the luscious flavors filled his senses. "This is good."

Abby smiled.

Leah laughed at his astonishment. "I told you."

"I'll listen to you next time." After taking another bite, he said, "You sound worried about Ruth."

He thought Leah might dissemble, but she nodded. "She refuses to tell me anything about where she goes other than to say she's with her friends."

"This is the secret you mentioned?"

"Ja."

"Have you asked her friends?"

"I tried asking Naomi Byler, but she was as closemouthed as Grossmammi. I want to believe everything is fine, but I can't when she clams up if I ask."

"Would you like me to follow her and see where she goes?" He gave Leah a mischievous smile and winked at Abby, who was listening intently. When his daughter grinned, he wanted to twirl her around the kitchen. "I can keep within the tree line. By now the trees around here and I are on a first-name basis, and she'd never see me."

Leah didn't return his grin. She toyed with a piece of her fried mush, but didn't eat it. "Don't be absurd, James."

"I didn't think I was."

"You were serious?" She lowered her fork. She clasped and unclasped her fingers on the tabletop as if she couldn't figure out what to do with her hands.

He resisted the urge to reach across the table and take her hands in his. "You're upset, and the way to ease your mind is to figure out what your grandmother is up to."

"She may not be 'up to' anything. Maybe Dorcas was right when she said Grossmammi is meeting with friends to make a quilt as a surprise for someone."

"If you think that, then why are you so bothered by this?"

"You never ask the easy questions, do you, professor?"

He was relieved that she was teasing him. Her natural curiosity and her love for her grandmother had her on edge, but her sense of humor was a saving grace.

"If you'd like, Leah, I'd be willing to follow her next Thursday evening. I've spent enough time among the trees on land with no trespassing signs to know how to keep out of sight."

"She'll have her buggy, and you won't be able to keep up." She laughed and shook her head. "What am I talking about? You don't need to stalk Grossmammi. If Dorcas is right, we'll look like fools."

"You don't believe Dorcas is right, do you?"

"I'd like to."

"You haven't asked me what I believe."

She regarded him with astonishment. "No, I haven't. What do you believe, James?"

"I believe," he said without a moment's hesitation, "that your grandmother is up to something, and it doesn't have anything to do with a quilt."

# 12

Leah bade James and Abby good night after each of them had a second serving of the fried mush, then watched while dad and daughter walked hand in hand out to the truck. She should go in and wash the dishes, so the kitchen didn't smell of the used oil, but she didn't want to let the evening end. To share her worries about her Grossmammi with James, who'd listened and didn't call them silly, had been wonderful. Seeing his joy when Abby greeted him joyfully made her own heart sing. She had lost count of the number of times she'd sent up prayers of thanks, but each one had been filled with gratitude for the blessings of being able to spend an evening with the Holdens.

She closed her eyes when she heard one door, then another, slam on the truck. The amazing interlude was over.

"Leah?"

Her eyes popped open, and she stared at James, who stood right in front of her. Lost in her thoughts, she hadn't heard him cross the yard.

His face was shadowed in the soft light coming from the kitchen, but nothing could smooth the masculine angles of his face. The dark rim of whiskers along his jaw emphasized its strong lines, teasing her fingers to explore. Their eyes met and held.

Unsure how long they stood so close, the silence cutting them off from the world, Leah didn't want to speak and ruin the wonder of their moment out of time.

"Abby left her box of crayons in the living room," James said.

The prosaic words ended the enchantment. Blinking as if waking from a dream, Leah said, "Let me get them." She stepped into the house.

At the same time, James said, "I'll get them." He grinned at her. "Great minds think alike."

"No, you stay here. I'll get the crayons."

She didn't wait to hear his response as she hurried through the kitchen and into the living room. Her heart thudded as if she'd run a marathon. Finding the box containing Abby's crayons, she held it close to her chest and forced her rapid breathing to slow.

Once she had herself under control, though her heart was still beating like rain on a metal roof, she went to James waiting on the porch. She offered him the box.

He took it and her hand and drew her to him. She stared at a button on the collar of his shirt. She didn't need to see his face to sense the intensity billowing from him.

She quivered as his fingers splayed across her back, pinning her to his firm chest. His hand rose to cup her head as he tilted her mouth under his. She gazed into his eyes, which glittered like twin stars in the sky above them. She saw the question there and heard it as if he'd spoken aloud. Did she know his lips ached for hers against them?

The decision was hers. Letting her choose was a gift nobody else had offered her. Instead Leah's life seemed to be constantly remolded to meet others' expectations. James was giving her the chance to make up her own mind. Would she listen to good sense, or would she listen to her heart?

Her fingers climbed his strong arms. Her breath became shallow when his finger caressed her ear, and she closed her eyes as she whispered his name. It was the invitation he needed. He claimed her mouth. She sensed his restraint as he explored her lips. She leaned into him, and his arms tightened around her as if he never wanted to release her.

Too soon he did. As he stepped back, she wanted to pull him

toward her. The night seemed cold and damp and lonely without his arms around her.

When he took her hand again, she watched, fascinated, as he raised it to his lips and pressed another kiss on her knuckles. He smiled, a silent promise letting her know he intended to find another chance to kiss her.

Then, taking the box of crayons, he walked to his truck, leaving her to stare after him, wondering if she'd made the best decision or the worst mistake of her life.

---

James sat by Abby's bed, holding a letter that had been waiting when they got home. He watched her sleeping, oblivious to the battles going on inside him.

He didn't regret giving into his need to kiss Leah tonight. Though he knew she was going to marry another man, he refused to let his one opportunity to taste her sweet lips pass him by. He was sure it could never happen again, and he'd hoped a kiss would dull the ache in him whenever he was with her and couldn't take her into his arms.

The kiss had the opposite effect, whetting his craving to kiss her again and again.

He should have known he was fooling himself. He wasn't a young teen with his first crush. He'd been in love before, and he still held his late wife in his heart where memories lived. He longed to spend now and the years yet to come with Leah. Pretending otherwise was stupid.

The paper crinkled in his hand, and Abby shifted on the bed.

Standing so he didn't wake her, he went into the small living room that was filled with piles of books. His and Abby's. He allowed himself a faint smile. His daughter had inherited his love of books and learning.

He glanced at the letter he held. The letter was from Bethel College in Kansas, one of the finest Mennonite colleges. He was being offered a full professorship in their biology department upon the completion of his PhD. It was everything he'd dreamed of when he began his postgraduate work.

It would mean a move from Stony Brook, which could be upsetting for Abby. It also meant that, even if Leah's grandmother convinced her to stay, he and his daughter would be gone. On the other hand, he wouldn't have to be in town to see her with Seth Eicher once they wed.

He dropped into the closest chair and stared at the letter without seeing it. He'd prayed for God's help. Was this the answer? A few weeks ago, it would have been what he wanted, a sure sign of God's forgiveness for his anger after the deaths that had collapsed his world.

Now he didn't know what to do about the letter and the job offer.

Leaning his head against the chair, he closed his eyes. How many times had he heard people say you should be careful what you pray for? He should have listened.

---

Leah was surprised to see Dorcas walking up the farm lane early the following Monday. It'd been almost a week since Leah had last had a chance to speak with her friend.

Too bad Leah couldn't share with her friend what was troubling her. Since James had kissed her, she hadn't seen him or Abby. She could think of far too many reasons why he was staying away, but none of them might be the truth. It might be as simple as he didn't need her to babysit.

Or he could be sorry he'd kissed her and didn't want to embarrass her by apologizing.

Though she had to keep her distressing thoughts to herself, Leah was glad to see her friend. Ruth had gone right after the midday meal to join her friends at Ida Mae and Vera Jean's house for a frolic. They planned to clean the house from top to bottom in preparation for the twins hosting the service on the next church Sunday. Though Leah had offered to help, Ruth had asked her to stay home and finish cooking the last of the tomatoes, turning them into sauce and canning them for use during the winter.

Leah had intended to do that once she finished putting the last loaves of bread into the oven. Slipping them in, she closed the door, set the timer, and turned as the redhead came into the kitchen.

"How are you?" Dorcas asked as she removed her black bonnet and hung it next to Leah's. "When I heard your Grossmammi was having a sisters' day, I thought I'd visit you."

"A sisters' day?" Leah asked, feigning humor. "More like a friends' day."

Dorcas giggled. "Not much difference. A sisters' day is when siblings get together to have a frolic. I think those four are closer than sisters."

"I agree." Leah resisted mentioning the other subject bothering her: What the quartet might be doing when they got together on Thursday evenings.

Her friend knew how concerned Leah was about Grossmammi's strange behavior. If Dorcas had heard anything to shed light on what Ruth was keeping as a secret, she would have told Leah straightaway.

"I made cinnamon rolls for breakfast," Leah continued. "There are a few left. Would you like a couple?"

"That sounds wunderbaar. I hurried through breakfast this morning because we had unplanned guests last night. A large tour group's bus broke down in the center of town. We had room for four of them. The others stayed at the hotel on the outskirts of Stony Brook, but came to join their friends for breakfast. Then I skipped lunch so I could get their rooms cleaned and ready for the next round of guests who are coming later this afternoon."

Bringing the plate of cinnamon rolls to the table, Leah whipped off the embroidered dishtowel and folded it. "Did you have enough food for the extra guests?"

"Barely." Dorcas sat across from Leah's usual seat. "If they'd been plain farmers instead of Englisch tourists, I wouldn't have had enough in spite of ordering plenty of food for the guests who have reservations for the weekend. I'm thankful two of the women were on diets and didn't want much more than a single egg and some fruit."

Leah laughed, a real laugh, at her friend's droll expression. If anyone could make food stretch, it was Dorcas Troyer.

"I can brew some Kaffi if you'd like," Leah said, "or would you prefer tea?"

"Tea is simpler. Let's have that. I know you've been as busy as I have." She gestured toward the counter where jars of the sauce they'd made that morning waited to be stored in the cellar. "Your Grossmammi is going to enjoy having all of that tomato sauce to use this winter. She's blessed you came to visit."

Leah smiled. Dorcas was one of the kindest people she'd ever met, and Leah was amazed that some young man hadn't asked her to be his wife. A few minutes later, they sat facing each other across the table. Leah let her stress ease while Dorcas entertained her with stories about the bed-and-breakfast's more eccentric guests. Leah wasn't sure if she laughed harder about the woman who insisted her three dogs be fed before she'd have breakfast herself or about the man who asked to have each part of his breakfast served on a separate plate and wouldn't allow the edges of the plates to touch.

"We meet all kinds," Dorcas said with her easy grin. "In fact, some of the people with the oddest idiosyncracies are my favorite guests because they're grateful that we do our best to make them comfortable."

"Myra is going to miss you when you get married and focus on taking care of your husband and family."

Dorcas's smile faded. "She's not going to have to worry any time soon."

"There's nobody special whom you've got your eye on?" Leah knew she was being nosy, but dear friends shared about courtships.

"Ja, but he's going to marry someone else."

"Oh, I'm sorry. It's got to be tough when the person you love doesn't love you back."

"Oh, he loves me, but he's going to marry someone else." Dorcas's voice shook on each word. "He feels obligated to his Grossdawdi, who—" She pressed her hands over her mouth before she could say more.

Leah guessed the truth anyway. "You're the one Seth is in love with, ain't so?"

Dorcas colored, her ears as crimson as Seth's had been when he'd hinted at being in love. "Leah, you know we don't talk about such things."

"Keeping the truth about the boy you're walking out with is fine when things go as planned, but it's wrong when it could mean an unhappy future for you, for him, and for me. You truly love him?"

"It doesn't matter, does it?"

"Love always matters. It's a cherished gift, something Jesus reminded His disciples of often. Besides, it matters to you, so it matters to me." She leaned forward and grasped Dorcas's hands. "You're my friend, and I don't want to see your heart broken because of a tradition started for who knows what reason."

"It's our way, Leah."

"I understand, but it isn't our way for one of us to make someone else unhappy when we can do something to help."

"There's nothing you can do. Seth is determined to please his Grossdawdi. He feels obligated to Perry, who took him and Willard in after their parents died. Many people commented on what a burden it was for a widower to be responsible for two young boys. Seth heard that and took the words to heart. As for Willard, I don't know what goes on in his head. He's always been a problem for Perry."

"If Seth were to explain to his Grossdawdi—"

"As I said, he feels a deep obligation to repay his Grossdawdi, and Perry has never asked anything of him before. Now Perry seems to have decided you'd make a *gut* wife for his grandson, and Seth sees this as a way to pay his debt to Perry."

Leah wanted to say Seth was being silly. Someone shouldn't make such an important decision based on what someone else wanted or because of a sense of obligation.

*Yet isn't that what I'm doing?* Leah wondered. If anyone other than Ruth suggested that Seth was Leah's perfect match, Leah would have ignored the matchmaking or insisted the matchmaker stop because it was clear to her that Seth and she didn't have good prospects for a happy life together.

Especially now that Leah knew he was in love with her friend.

*So why am I not announcing to the whole world that I won't marry Seth?* Leah asked herself.

*Because Grossmammi wants me to marry her neighbor's grandson, and I feel obligated to Grossmammi for being there when Mamm died as well as for teaching me about herbs.* She couldn't fault Seth when she was acting the same way. There had to be a way to fix what was about to become a debacle. She respected Seth, and she cared too much about Dorcas to come between them.

*Then I could look to a future with James.*

No, she must not let such thoughts escape the secret recesses of her heart. She didn't want to think about a time when she wouldn't see James or Abby again, but what future was there for the three of them?

She needed to focus on what she could to do help her friends now. That would be the best way to ignore her complicated longings.

"Dorcas, you and I are two intelligent women." She folded her arms on the table. "Let's find a way to bring you and Seth together without making him feel as if he's let his Grossdawdi down."

"Danki, Leah." Dorcas's shy smile lit her face. "Ask, and I'll try to help you with the guy you love."

"That's kind of you, but I don't know if there's anything you can do."

Her friend's eyes widened. "Because you left your *Liebling* at home?"

Instead of answering, Leah grasped Dorcas's hands and squeezed them. Lowering her voice to a conspiratorial whisper, she said, "I suggest you become very, *very* interested in seeing Seth's new beehive. Maybe if Perry sees you and Seth together, he'll realize you are best wife for his grandson."

"Oh, danki, Leah!" Happy tears bubbled into Dorcas's eyes. "You have no idea how much this means to me."

"I think I do, and if I didn't, your smile would tell me."

"Please let me return the favor. I've got family in Lancaster County too. One of them might know the young man you're sweet on. They could give him a nudge in the right direction toward you."

"It's better to focus on taking care of one problem at a time, ain't so?"

Dorcas considered, then nodded. "I'm sure you're right, but don't think I'll forget that I owe you a great favor."

"No more talk of favors. That's what's led to this complicated situation."

She smiled as Dorcas began to ask questions about Seth's newest hive and anything else Leah had learned about bees. Answering as best she could, Leah was glad she didn't have to ask aloud a question of her own.

*What would Dorcas say if I admitted I'm falling in love with an Englischer?*

# 13

Leah dreamed that she walked through Upper Falls Park once more with James. This time, they walked hand in hand, not worrying if anyone took note of an Englisch man and a plain woman holding hands. Not that anyone was around. Not even Abby. It was the two of them, Leah and James, standing close to the waterfall which was cascading over the rocks and creating the ethereal rainbows in the air.

A cry of dismay broke into her lovely vision.

Fighting her way out of the cobwebs of sleep, Leah regretted how the dream vanished. She had been able to force herself—with some success—to stop thinking about James during the day, but images of him filled her dreams every night. She couldn't control them, though she'd tried. Nor could she escape the sense of loss when she woke and realized she was torturing herself. She had no idea how to banish the dreams filled with love and happiness.

"Leah!"

Ruth calling her name snapped her out of her self-pity. Jumping to her feet, she grabbed her bathrobe from the door. A glance at the window showed it must be close to dawn. The moon was near the western horizon.

She pulled the robe around her, tying it in place, as she hurried down the stairs.

"Grossmammi?" she called through the darkness.

"In the kitchen!" came back a harried answer.

"What's wrong?" She tossed her braid over her shoulder as she went into the dim kitchen. She would have run into the table if she hadn't become familiar with the room. As it was, she bumped against one of the chairs.

*Why hadn't Grossmammi turned on the lamp?*

"The garden."

Reaching to turn on the propane lamp hanging from the ceiling, Leah started to ask why Ruth was upset, then she looked out the window over the sink. It gave her a clear view of the garden. She saw the glitter of ice crystals in the last of the moonlight. She hadn't guessed the temperature would plummet in the early hours before dawn, but it had.

Leah urged Ruth to bring every bucket and any deep pots in the cupboard. While the older woman bent to gather those, Leah grabbed her coat and a scarf to throw over her hair. She jammed her feet into her boots at the same time she opened the door.

She groped along the house to find the hose. It was connected to the outdoor tap. Turning the water on, she ran on the crackling grass to where Ruth was coming out with a trio of buckets and the big Dutch oven.

"I'll fill these," Leah said.

"Take this." Ruth pressed a flashlight in Leah's hand before she went into the house to get more containers.

Switching on the flashlight, Leah tossed icy vegetables into the buckets and pots. There were so many still to pick. She left what she'd gathered and ran to the porch, throwing open the cupboard. She took out the baskets she'd used before for harvesting the vegetables. If they could pick all the beans and peas and peppers before the sun rose along with the temperature, they might be able to save them.

It became a race against the sunrise while Leah went along the row and snapped off every bean. Ruth did the same where she'd planted peas. As soon as her basket was filled, Leah rushed to drop the vegetables in cold water. She did the same with Grossmammi's baskets. She moaned when light flashed across the garden, and then she realized it was James's truck. Was it so close to sunrise? Her aching back warned she'd been working in the garden for nearly two hours.

"What are you doing?" James asked as he led Abby across the yard.

"Trying to save as much of the garden as we can," Leah answered. "We need to get the vegetables picked before the sun comes up."

"What can I do to help?"

"Bring more of those empty baskets," Leah called as she kept plucking the beans and tossing them into the container beside her. "There should be some in the laundry room cupboard."

Her fingertips burned with the cold, but she paid no attention to the discomfort as she continued working. When James returned with more baskets—smaller ones Ruth must have used for taking food to fund-raising events or to Sunday services—Leah thanked him but didn't stop breaking off the beans.

"What else can I do?"

"Take these filled baskets over there." Leah pointed to where water ran from the hose. "Rinse the vegetables in cold water."

"Cold water? Why not hot?"

"The change in temperature would be too shocking for the vegetables." She looked at him for a moment with a grim smile. "You wouldn't want to be cold and dropped into a hot bath, would you?"

"A warm bath sounds good about now."

Before she could reply, he took the baskets from beside her and Ruth, and carried them to the hose spilling water through the grass. He sprayed the beans, shaking the basket to make sure each vegetable got soaked. Dumping the beans into a bucket, he paused long enough to let Abby into the house.

Nobody spoke as they worked to save as much as they could. They ignored the pumpkins, which they hoped, for Abby's sake, would be able to handle a single night of below-freezing temperatures.

Dawn seeped across the yard and reached under the trees to dance on the frost atop the plants. As Ruth called for a halt because it was too late to save anything more, Leah looked around and smiled despite her exhaustion. They'd picked everything except for one small section of peppers. Those might be all right if she got them into cold water and then parboiled them while she was making breakfast.

When James stepped forward to assist Ruth into the house, Leah was grateful. He returned a few minutes later to help Leah drain the cold water out of several buckets and carry the shrunken vegetables into the kitchen. Urging her to do what she needed to in order to save the harvest, he rushed outside to collect the rest of the containers. He brought in the vegetables and placed them in the sink where the others waited.

He poured a cup of coffee and carried it to where Grossmammi sat, her shoulders slumped. Setting it in front of her, he asked, "Do you want milk and sugar, Ruth?"

"Both," she answered. "Lots of sugar. Maybe it'll get me going for the day."

Leah asked when James passed her at the stove to get milk from the fridge, "Can you stay for breakfast?"

"I wish I could. I need to get going, or I'll be late for my first class."

Only then did she realize he wore a tie. His shoes were scuffed, and dampness had left stains on the hems of his slacks. When she started to apologize for his clothes, he waved her to silence.

"I keep telling my students they have to be ready to do fieldwork at any time." He smiled as he lifted the milk. "This should give them a good laugh."

Leah set the Dutch oven on the burner to get water boiling. As she sorted peppers out of the sink so she could drop them into the pot, she watched James put the milk next to where Ruth sat.

He went around the table and gave Abby a kiss on the top of her head and told her to be a good girl. With a wave, he hurried out. The sound of his truck's engine was preternaturally loud in the morning quiet.

Making a quick breakfast of oatmeal and home fries allowed Leah to keep an eye on the other pots on the stove. Ruth was as silent as Abby during the meal, which surprised Leah. Other than thanking Leah for serving breakfast, the older woman said nothing until the little girl had finished and went outside to check the pumpkins.

Ruth pushed herself to her feet, opened a drawer, and pulled out a knife. She began to cut the ends off the beans while Leah scooped the last of the peppers out of the boiling water and set them to one side. If they didn't turn black as they cooled, they would be edible.

Scooping out a large bowl of peapods, Leah set it on the table. She got a colander from the cupboard, set it on her lap, and reached for a pod to begin shelling.

"James is a truly *gut* man," Ruth said without preamble. "I understand why you offered to help him. He pitched in to help us without waiting to be asked."

Leah looked up from shucking peas and dropping them into the colander. "You sound surprised."

"No, not surprised. Not in the least, because his daughter is a well-behaved Kind. Though I have to say I'm delighted to see her eyes twinkling with mischief."

"I don't think any little one should behave all the time."

Ruth chuckled, but it sounded forced.

Putting down the pods she was holding, Leah stood so she could meet Ruth's eyes. "*Was iss letz?*"

"Nothing is wrong. At least, not yet, but I want you to remember that as nice a man as James Holden is, he's an Englischer."

Leah sighed, but didn't let her gaze waver. If Grossmammi knew about the dream she'd interrupted this morning, the conversation would have taken a different turn.

"I know that," Leah said, keeping her voice calm, "and so does James." She didn't add that her heart wasn't as willing to accept that fact.

Ruth grasped Leah by the shoulders and said, "I don't want to see you get hurt. I wouldn't want you to have a single day when you weren't happy." She smiled sadly. "That is every Grossmammi's wish for her *Kinskinder*."

Leah hugged Ruth, then forced herself to smile as Abby came into the house. Turning her attention to the little girl, Leah sensed Ruth's anxiety. The older woman was worried about Leah, and Leah knew she had a reason to be. Until Leah could convince her heart to accept good sense, the danger of being hurt was enormous.

---

James smiled as he swung Abby into her car seat. As she did most days, Leah was giving him highlights of the time she'd spent with his daughter. There hadn't been any new breakthroughs for Abby, but she smiled when Leah spoke to her. For that, he was grateful.

Abby opened the book she'd been carrying when she came out of the house. It was one of the Amish primers Leah was using to teach his daughter what she was missing at school. He noted the size of the font on the open pages, and he guessed that, with Leah's help, Abby was moving ahead of her peers.

It was another debt he owed to the wonderful woman who loved Abby as if she were her own.

Taking a slip of bright-green paper from the seat, he held it out to Leah.

"What's this?" she asked.

"It's the announcement of a program at Eastern Indiana Mennonite College. I thought you might want to go with me tomorrow."

"To the college?" Her voice took on the sound of a wistful child's staring at packages under a Christmas tree.

He hadn't been wrong when he'd suspected she longed to study more formally than she could from her grandmother and from books.

Tapping the page, he said, "Dr. Rhonda Duncan is giving a lecture on her latest research."

"Oh, I just finished reading her latest book!" Leah's eyes sparkled with exhilaration. "I'm fascinated with her insight into introducing certain herbs into the diets of seniors to help keep their minds more alert."

He smiled. "I noticed you had several books by her, and when I saw a poster announcing her lecture, I thought you'd be interested."

"I'd love to attend." Her face fell as she glanced at the house. "I shouldn't."

"Why not? I know Amish value informal learning throughout their lives. This isn't a class. It's a presentation on the findings from her latest research." He forced himself to add, "Your grandmother is welcome to come too, if that would make it easier."

"I'm not sure she would consider going."

"Why not?"

She clasped her hands behind her and turned to look at the barn. "You don't understand."

"Then explain it to me. Does your grandmother dislike me?"

"No!" She faced him again, and the glow was gone from her pretty eyes. "She doesn't dislike you, James."

"But?"

"She dislikes the idea of me spending so much time with you. It's not because of anything you've done or said."

"It's because of what I am, isn't it?"

She sighed. "It has more to do with what *I* am. An Amish woman shouldn't spend as much time with an Englischer as I do with you, James."

"Yes, you'd spend the twenty minutes alone with me each way in the car, but the lecture is going to have at least a hundred people attending it. Plain folks and non-plain folks. I think you'd enjoy hearing Rhonda Duncan."

"I do want to hear her." She sighed. "Let me discuss it with Grossmammi."

"And if she says you can't go?"

"Then I won't go. Wait here. I'll be right back."

James called her name, and she faced him. He'd seen her unbridled excitement at the chance to hear the lecture. He wanted her to have that opportunity.

"Leah, I was serious. Tell your grandmother that she's welcome to come to the lecture too. I'm sure she'd be as interested to hear Rhonda's presentation as you are."

Emotions paraded through her eyes. Excitement, relief, and what seemed to be disappointment. The last startled—and pleased—him. Was it possible that she was bothered by his offer to take her grandmother too? It was wrong, but he hoped Leah wanted to spend time with just him.

"Danki," she said before going toward the house.

He watched until she vanished through the door. He admired how much respect she showed her grandmother, but he didn't want Leah to miss the chance to hear a speaker who was renowned in the field of herbal healing.

He wanted to spend an evening with Leah. No Abby and no Ruth—though he wasn't sure about the latter. He and Leah could listen to a presentation and then discuss it on the way home. He doubted Leah would have other opportunities to attend such a program if she married Seth Eicher, who seemed content to expand his interests no farther than his bees flew.

James leaned against the truck and watched the house, waiting for Leah to return. If she told him that her grandmother refused to give her permission to go, should he push? Ruth knew their plain world far better than James could. Was his invitation a mistake? He could be putting her into an untenable situation.

He'd misread the situation with Connie. He hadn't seen a single sign that she'd considered committing suicide. The morning of the day she died, Connie had been talking about a possible clinical trial her doctor had suggested her for. It could have been the answer to beating her cancer, the true answer to a prayer.

Why had he focused on her optimism and failed to notice her despair? He hadn't speculated about her state of mind, believing everything she told him. How could he have been so wrong?

Was he also wrong in asking Leah to go to the lecture? *No.* It might be the most foolish thing he'd ever done, but he'd regret it if he didn't try to have one evening with her. Just the two of them without family obligations intruding.

The door opened, and Leah emerged. When he saw her smile, he couldn't hide his own grin, knowing her answer before she told him. Her grandmother had agreed for her to attend.

"This once," Leah added.

He nodded, knowing Ruth was being magnanimous to agree to Leah taking a single excursion with him. Ruth's love for her granddaughter must have overridden her concern about Leah driving to the college and back with just him.

"Good," he said. "I'll pick you up around five. That'll give us plenty of time if there's traffic."

"I'll plan on an early supper."

Before he could halt them, words he shouldn't have said popped out of his mouth. "Let me take you out to the new restaurant in Stony Brook after the lecture."

She hesitated, and he was sure she was going to say no. It would prove what he knew. She had more good sense than he did.

"Do they serve Cincinnati chili?" she asked, surprising him.

"No. The place I get that for Myra is in Oxford, Ohio. So will you let me take you to dinner tomorrow night?"

She raised her eyes and met his gaze. He saw her uncertainty and, stronger than any other emotion, her eagerness to spend an evening with him without Abby or her grandmother.

"Ja," she whispered, and smiled before she rushed into the house.

He grinned. Yes, he was being a fool because he was getting in deeper, but it was too late to turn back, even if he wanted to.

# 14

Though Ruth had given her permission to attend the lecture with James, Leah felt as if she were sneaking out of the house like a teenager enjoying the first taste of Rumspringa. But she wasn't a child. She was a grown woman who was looking forward to attending what James assured her would be an illuminating lecture. Nothing more.

She almost laughed at her ridiculous thoughts. James was more to her than a friend, so she wasn't surprised when Ruth gave her a dubious frown as she tied her black bonnet over her Kapp in preparation for his arrival.

If Leah had been a teenager, she might have asked why Ruth was acting chilly. Grossmammi had had her chance to put the kibosh on the plans. At the time, Ruth's agreement had been the definition of reluctance, but she'd agreed. She obviously regretted her decision now.

Changing her mind and not attending the lecture with James would have resolved the problem, but Leah couldn't bring herself to cancel. She was looking forward to the lecture by one of her favorite authors almost as much as enjoying the evening with James.

"When will you be back?" Ruth asked, looking at the book she held. It was a book on herbs Leah had brought with her from Pennsylvania.

"The lecture is scheduled to last two hours. We plan to stop for dinner on the way home."

Ruth's frown deepened. "Be careful, Leah. I fear that you're getting in over your head with this Englischer. That is why, after considering your request again, I don't think it's a *gut* idea for you to go. You're a grown woman, though, and these decisions are yours to make."

"I know tonight can't be repeated, and I also know James and I can be no more than friends."

That was the wrong thing to say because Ruth sat straighter, put down the book, and scowled at Leah.

"'No more than friends?' Does that mean you've considered becoming more? You're Amish, and he's an Englischer."

"I never forget that." She hated the idea of having to choose her words with care while speaking with the older woman. She'd always been able to confide in Grossmammi, and she didn't want that to change.

She didn't want a lot to change—including the time she spent with James. Hoping she could continue to try to bridge their two worlds was absurd. She prayed God would put the direction He wished her to go into her heart.

What if following God's will removed James and Abby from her life?

As if she'd asked aloud, Ruth said, "We Amish agree to remain separate from the world. Going out for tonight with James, who is a *gut* man in spite of the whispers about his wife's death, is a mistake. No matter how innocent he is in the events leading to that poor woman's accident, he's an Englischer."

"Please trust me."

The frustration left Ruth's voice. "I do trust you, Leah. However, I know what it's like to be young and believe you can handle whatever life tosses your way. You're old enough to begin baptism classes and join the Leit. After that, you can marry and live the life you've been raised to follow."

"I understand."

She did understand, but she also knew how she found it more and more impossible to ignore the twin longings bursting from her heart and from her mind. The longing to learn more about botany in classes like the ones James taught was almost as strong as her yearning to be in his arms.

"Seth is taking baptismal classes now," Ruth said.

"He told me."

"He'll be looking to settle down with a wife."

Leah nodded, not wanting to reveal she intended to help Seth see that Dorcas was the perfect wife for him. If his marriage would make his Grossdawdi happy, then what better solution was there than for Seth to marry the woman he loved and who loved him?

The sound of James's truck gave Leah the excuse to put an end to the strained conversation. How could she have told Grossmammi of her plans to help Dorcas when Ruth was so set on Leah marrying Seth? Again, Leah wanted to ask why. Did Ruth believe it was the way to keep one member of her distant family in Stony Brook, or was there another reason Leah hadn't considered?

Kissing the older woman's wrinkled cheek, Leah said, "When I get home, I'll tell you everything I learned about herbs."

"Make sure that's all you learn about tonight."

Heat slapped Leah's face, but she nodded. No matter how much Ruth asserted that she trusted her granddaughter, Leah wondered if she did.

She also wondered if Ruth was right to be worried. Her pulse gave an exultant leap as she walked out to see James getting out of the truck.

---

Leah couldn't stop talking about how amazing the lecture was. She knew she was babbling as they returned to Stony Brook, but the whole experience of sitting in a lecture hall and listening to the information shared by one of her favorite authors seemed like a dream come true.

When she paused and began to apologize for her exuberance, James chuckled. "I'm glad you enjoyed the program. You were a sponge, Leah, soaking up information."

"Danki for inviting me. It was wunderbaar."

"The college sponsors regular programs like tonight's. If I see something else I think you'd be interested in, I'll let you know."

"Danki," she repeated, though she knew how unlikely it was that she'd ever attend another lecture at the college. As much as she'd upset Ruth with what she'd assured her was a one-time event, she couldn't imagine putting the older woman through such distress again.

The sign welcoming them to Stony Brook flashed in the truck's headlights. They turned onto Main Street, passing dimly lit shops. The pizza shop and the Chinese restaurant glowed in the starlight.

Halfway along the street, James flipped the turn signal and pulled the truck into the parking lot of a long, low building set behind a well-lit sign announcing it was Antonio's Cucina.

"Do you like Italian food?" James asked as he parked the truck at the rear of the crowded lot.

"Spaghetti is one of my favorites. We serve it often at fund-raiser dinners."

"What kind of fund-raising?"

"If a family has a financial need, like medical bills or a fire, we have a dinner. Everyone is invited, plain and Englisch. Everything is donated, and the money goes to the family. They're popular because the Leit likes to help its members, and everyone enjoys a chance to get out and see everybody else while enjoying a *gut* meal."

Switching off the engine, he motioned for her to stay where she was. "I'll get your door."

"I'm capable of opening—"

"Let me be a gentleman tonight, Leah, and treat you the way a lady should be treated." He grinned as he stepped out. "It's the least I can do when you've never complained about the short notice I've given you when I need you to take care of Abby." Before he closed the door, he added, "Like I need you to tomorrow."

Leah laughed as he walked around the truck and opened her door. "I'm happy to watch Abby tomorrow." She got out of the truck and moved aside so he could close the door. "You didn't have to go through all that to ask me."

"It was fun, though, wasn't it?"

"I'd say the word you're looking for is funny."

"Ouch!" He put his hand to his chest and reeled as if wounded. "Here I'm trying to be debonair and charming, and you think I'm being funny."

"Aren't you?"

Grinning, he nodded. "Yes, but if we keep standing here in the parking lot, we'll miss our reservation."

As she started toward the restaurant, he touched her shoulder. A frisson of delight raced through her like a storm wind. The ability to move, to draw in a breath, deserted her as he took her hand and settled it on his crooked arm.

"James, we shouldn't . . ." She glanced at her fingers on his dark sleeve.

He sighed and lowered his arm. "You're right. Giving the Stony Brook gossips more to talk about would be silly." His lips tipped in a tongue-in-cheek grin. "I'm feeling sort of like I did the night I went to my junior prom with a girl I had a huge crush on. I don't think I said more than two words on the way from her house to the high school."

"I hope you plan to say more than a couple of words during dinner."

"Let me start now. You look lovely."

She glanced at the rose-colored dress she wore, for once without a black apron. "You've seen this dress before."

"I wasn't talking about the dress. I'm talking about you. You look lovely."

"I look the same as I always do."

His smile softened. "I agree, and you always look lovely."

"James..."

Chuckling, he said, "Okay, I know you Amish don't like to be complimented, but is it a compliment when it's a fact that God added extra beauty to your face and your kind heart?"

"Ja. We shouldn't parade the gifts God granted us. We should use them for His glory."

He held up his hands. "I get it. You Amish don't like being complimented."

"Oh, I like it as much as anyone else, I guess. But we try to limit compliments so we don't give into Hochmut."

"Pride?" He chuckled. "My *Deitsch* vocabulary has grown since I met you."

"And I've learned more about trees than I'll ever need to know."

"An inescapable side effect of hanging out with an arborist." He held the door for her. "You've taught me a lot about herbs. I should ask you if you'll share the recipe for your knee-scrape tincture. I've used almost the whole bottle."

"I hadn't noticed Abby had hurt herself."

"Not her. Me. I've been collecting samples of bark, and my knuckles look like I've rubbed them against a grater. Your tincture dampens the pain."

Leah was about to tell him that she'd be glad to give him the recipe, but instead she stared at the room they'd entered.

A single votive candle burned in the center of each table covered with a white tablecloth. The paintings on the barn-wood walls depicted buildings, which Leah guessed could be found around Stony Brook. Beneath her feet, the slate floor was as smooth as a mirror.

The hostess, wearing black trousers and a white shirt, showed them to a table near one of the windows with a view of the square built around a gazebo. Or was it a bandstand? She'd heard about those in Midwestern towns, but wasn't sure what they looked like.

Leah murmured her thanks when the hostess handed her a menu. She hoped the woman realized her gratitude was not only for the menu, but for the way the hostess treated her as if she were just another customer and didn't stare at her Kapp or ask awkward questions. The hostess took their drink orders and said their waiter would be over in a few minutes.

Opening the menu, Leah squinted to read the tiny print.

"Allow me." James offered his cell phone that glowed like an electric light. "I've heard the lasagna here is the best in Indiana."

Closing her menu, she said, "Then that's what I'll have."

When a dark-haired waiter brought their sodas, James asked, "Okay if I order for us?"

"Go ahead."

Placing an order for two servings of the lasagna, two side salads with the house Italian dressing and some mozzarella garlic bread, he handed the menus to the waiter, who took them and went to put in their order.

"I want to say danki again," Leah said, clasping her hands on the table. "The program was inspiring. It made me want to learn more."

"Inspiring and motivating students are the goals of a good teacher." He leaned toward her, folding his arms on the table. "My favorite part of teaching is when I see a student's eyes light up. Then I know they've grasped the concept I've been teaching."

"Have you always wanted to be a professor?"

"I knew I wanted to study trees from the time when I was seven or eight, and when I realized I could share my zeal on the subject, teaching seemed like the right way to spend my life."

"It's taken you so many years to learn how to teach?" She smiled. "Our teachers learn from each other and jump in with both feet."

"I'm older than most other PhD candidates. They usually go from college to graduate school and then on to postgrad work without a break. I didn't."

"Why?"

He shifted in his chair. "I took a semester off after my wife died."

Leah reached across the table and touched his hand. "I'm sorry. I should have guessed. I know you, and I know you wanted to spend time with Abby."

"I would rather you ask. Too many people tiptoe around the subject of Connie's death. I'm sure you've heard the rumors."

"I have, but I figure gossip is worth what it costs to get—nothing. I'm sorry you've had to deal with that."

He settled his hand over hers. "Thanks, but I've learned to ignore it. There are as many theories of why the accident happened as there are people who figure they know. The sheriff believes Connie drove off the road, striking a fence." His eyes grew moist. "Too often when I try to go to sleep, I see that white paint from the fence and the dents on the car. She overcompensated and turned too hard in the other direction, and that's when she went off the road and struck a tree. Connie said she was determined her cancer wouldn't kill her. She was like that. Fearless and stubborn. I never guessed her words would prove true as they did."

Leah sat back as the waiter brought their salads. She shook her head when he offered freshly ground pepper, not sure she could trust her voice to speak.

As soon as the waiter left, Leah whispered, "I'm sorry, James. I shouldn't have brought this up."

"You didn't. I did." He gave her a weak grin. "No matter what you think, it does feel good to talk about Connie. Others change the subject when I mention her name. I don't want her final act—if the accident wasn't accidental—to be the way she's remembered when she was so much more. Abby reminds me of her more every day with her creativity and her gentle heart. When she smiled—" He pulled a handkerchief out of his pocket and dabbed his eyes. "Sorry."

"Why do you feel you must apologize? She was your wife and the mother of your child. If you didn't miss her, there would be something wrong with you."

Holding her hand between his broader ones, he asked, "Has anyone told you, Leah Kauffman, that you've got a gift for saying the right thing at the right time?"

With a laugh, she shook her head. "Usually I open my mouth before I've thought through what I'm going to say."

"I haven't seen that."

"So you'll be finished soon with your college work?" she asked, wanting to turn the conversation away from herself. Picking up her fork, she speared a slice of cucumber in her salad bowl.

He nodded. "In the spring, and then I have to decide if I want to stay teaching at Eastern Indiana Mennonite College or look for another position."

"And leave Stony Brook?" She was proud of how calm her voice sounded.

"It's not my first choice, but there are other parts of the country I would like to see." He gave her a teasing smile. "Maybe Lancaster County in Pennsylvania."

Leah lowered her head before he could see how pleased she was.

She couldn't help imagining showing him around the hills and along the creeks and streams of the farmlands where she'd grown up.

After taking another bite of salad, she asked, "Anywhere else?"

"Plenty. I saw amazing places I'd like to revisit while I was with the army."

Shock exploded through Leah. As her fingers grew numb, she tightened her grip on the fork so it didn't fall and clatter on the table. She must have heard him wrong. He'd told her that he was a Mennonite, and even a liberal Mennonite was charged, as the Amish were, with finding a life of pacifism and believing in turning the other cheek as Jesus taught during His sermon on the mount.

"The United States Army?" she managed to choke out. "Did I hear you right?" She prayed he would tell her she'd misunderstood.

---

When he saw the color vanish from Leah's face, James pushed aside his salad bowl and reached across the table for her hands. Her fingers trembled as he wrapped his around them.

"Are you okay, Leah?" he asked.

Her wide eyes drilled into him. "You were—did you say the United States Army?"

"Yes, I spent time with the army."

"I see." Drawing her hands out of his, she stood. "I need to go home now."

He got up too, abruptly worried. Her face had no more color than the tablecloth. "Are you okay? Do you feel ill?"

"Please, James. Take me home now."

He was aware of the other diners turning to watch them. This time it wasn't the innocent curiosity he'd seen when he came into the restaurant with Leah. Now they were wondering why an Amish woman was staring at him with tears glittering in her eyes.

The sight pierced him so deeply he had to fight not to recoil in pain. He yearned to comfort her and have those tears vanish as her eyes crinkled with one of her stunning smiles. Maybe she'd understand if he explained.

"Leah—"

"I need to go." She rushed toward the door, almost running into the hostess, who was leading other guests toward a table.

Pausing long enough to pull out his wallet and toss enough money on the table to cover their meal and a tip, James followed. He burst out of the restaurant and looked in both directions. Where was she?

A shadow moved near his truck. *Leah!*

James strode toward her and started to speak.

She stopped him by saying, "Please don't speak. I just want to go home."

"All right," he replied, though he knew it was a mistake. "I'll take you home."

"Danki, James."

Those were the last words she spoke on the way to her grandmother's farm. He tried twice to restart the conversation but failed.

Leah jumped out before the truck came to a complete stop. She ran to the house and was inside before he could move.

Twisting the wheel so hard the tires squealed, James drove back toward the road. He gripped the wheel as though he wanted to drive his fingers right through it. When he pulled into own driveway and turned off the engine, he didn't open the truck's door. Instead, he slammed his fists on the steering wheel before leaning his head against it.

She hadn't gotten sick. She'd been fleeing the truth she hadn't wanted to hear. The truth about why he'd lost his faith along with his wife and best friend.

He'd made a mess of everything. Talking with Leah had been so easy, and he'd let down his guard to tell her about the secrets he'd been keeping, secrets that gnawed at his soul. Instead of the truth bringing them closer, he'd sent her fleeing. If he'd told her carefully, leading up to the truth slowly, would it have made a difference? If she'd given him a chance to explain . . .

Or was there no explanation he could give without upsetting her more? If he could find a way, would she agree to listen to him? He'd thought she was a good friend, someone he could trust with the truth. A good friend? He knew that kind of relationship with Leah wouldn't be enough for him, but it must be. She was Amish and was most likely going to marry Seth Eicher. The smart thing would be walking away, knowing he and Leah could never have been more than friends. But how could he when Leah had become such a vital part of his life?

He needed help.

"God," he whispered, "I know You haven't heard from me in a long time, but I pray You'll listen to me tonight. Help me. If You can't help me, please help Leah. Don't let me be the reason she marries the wrong man."

# 15

The lamp glowed in the kitchen when Leah entered the Kauffman farmhouse. Ruth sat at the table, mending the pocket on an apron. Leah wasn't surprised Ruth had waited up to talk with her.

"How was your evening, Leah?"

"The lecture was wunderbaar." It seemed as if the program had taken place in someone else's life. Someone who believed it was possible for an Amish woman to fall in love with an Englischer and think they could make a life together.

James Holden wasn't the man she'd believed him to be. What other disturbing secrets had he kept from her? The thought threatened to dissolve her into tears.

"Afterward?" prompted Ruth.

"We went to a restaurant."

"Which didn't go wunderbaar."

"No." Leah added nothing else, because there really wasn't anything else to say.

"I'm sorry."

Leah was almost as shocked at her Grossmammi's sympathy as she was with James's announcement. "I didn't think you wanted me to go to the restaurant."

"What I want is far less important than what God wants for you, Liebling."

She set her bonnet on the peg. "Grossmammi, I wish I knew what that was."

"We all do."

Leah walked to the table and sat across from Ruth. Folding her arms, she said, "You always know what God wants you to do."

The older woman smiled. "My dear Kind, nobody can be certain what God has planned for any of us. That's why we call it faith. We have to believe that what we've learned and how we've lived gives us the tools we need to make the best possible decision when we reach a crossroad. Left or right? Forward or back? Which way do we want to go? Which way does God expect us to go? What if the answers aren't the same? It's then we must turn to faith and prayer, and trust that God will make His plan plain to us."

"How about when it isn't?"

"Have faith the answer will become clear, and you'll know within your heart what God expects of you. One thing I've learned in the years I've lived is never to doubt that an answer will come. I need to believe it will and that I can accept the answer when it does."

"What if that answer doesn't take me where I planned to go?"

"God's will must come first. If you fight it, you'll never have peace in your life. Only you can decide what to do. You asked me earlier if I trusted you. I do trust you to make the right decision." She smiled sadly. "Whatever it is."

---

James was exhausted. It had been a long day at the university, being quizzed by his adviser about his thesis's conclusions. They had done several of these practice sessions for the orals he'd have in another few months, but this one hadn't gone well because of how often he'd let his mind wander to Abby and Leah, and how

Ruth had been the one to come out to get his daughter when he dropped Abby off. He didn't need a neon sign to let him know Leah was avoiding him.

He appreciated Neil's assistance because he knew he would fail without rehearsing the possible questions he might face when defending his thesis. Not many professors were as interested in the success of their grad students as Neil Judd was, and Neil had become even more of a taskmaster after James showed him the job offer he'd received. Neil interspersed long sessions of focusing on the minutiae of James's thesis with good humor and anecdotes of his own experiences before he was awarded his own PhD in botany.

Even so, the long hours of having to recall every detail in his almost three-hundred-page thesis took their toll. Some days, like today, it seemed as if Neil knew more about what James had written than James did himself.

"I should have put in fewer facts," James had grumbled at the end of the third hour of the grilling.

Neil's response had been a booming laugh, so infectious James had to give in and chuckle too. It'd been an idiotic statement because a PhD thesis was about presenting an idea and then developing the argument to support it with a multitude of facts.

"Go home," Neil finally told him. Giving an indifferent wave that contradicted his easy smile, his advisor had said, "If I wear out your brain now, you won't have any left to defend your thesis."

"It may be too late." He'd rubbed his eyes that were sandy with exhaustion. "My brain feels like a serving of fried mush."

"Fried mush?" He stuck out his tongue and made a gagging sound. "That sounds horrible."

"It's surprisingly tasty."

"Where did you eat it?"

"My babysitter is Amish, and she insisted I try it. Like I said, despite its horrible name, it was good."

The realization hit James that knowing Leah had changed him in ways he hadn't noticed. Before he'd met her, he wouldn't have had any idea there was something called fried mush. Now the words slipped past his lips readily.

The thought had been followed by a pulse of pain when he remembered how he'd made a mess of their one and only date. If he'd been honest with her from the start...

Then she might have refused to watch Abby. None of them would have had the chance to learn more about each other. He wanted her to know everything about him the way he longed to know everything about her. If she had let him finish telling her about his experiences, maybe she wouldn't have reacted as she did.

Or maybe she would have.

As James drove away from the college, he feared he'd never know because he suspected that, when he picked up Abby tonight, Leah would have an excuse why she wouldn't be able to watch her any longer. Of course, that assumed she would speak to him. Her reasoning would be kind and honest, but she would avoid the truth of how a few words about his past had ruined everything they'd shared.

Feeling as though he'd been flayed, he wondered if God had heard his prayer. Why should He? James had railed against Him as tragedy took over his life.

*Our Lord taught us to forgive one another as He forgives us.* James remembered Leah saying that when she first came to the bed-and-breakfast.

She believed those words. Could he?

A motion beyond the crossroad caught his eyes, halting his soul-searching.

A buggy driving in the same direction he was headed.

He squinted to see through the deep twilight. Not just any buggy. It was a buggy being pulled by Ruth Kauffman's horse. He recognized it in the lights from her buggy. He hadn't seen another brown horse with patches of white on its front two legs around Stony Brook.

He considered pulling even with the buggy and giving Ruth a wave, though he wondered if she'd acknowledge him. Had Leah told her grandmother about their disastrous date? Maybe he should let her go on her way while he turned toward the Kauffman farm to retrieve Abby.

Suddenly he remembered. It was Thursday. The evening Ruth told Leah she spent time with her friends.

None of them lived in the direction Ruth was driving. The elderly twins' house and Naomi's farm were on the far side of Stony Brook.

James was glad the stop sign gave him an excuse to sit and watch while Ruth's buggy continued along the road away from him. He didn't take his foot off the brake as he watched her turn. She drove toward the Eichers' farmhouse.

Glancing at the clock on the dash, he saw it was the time when Ruth went to visit her friends each Thursday evening. So why was she going to the Eicher farm?

Knowing he should turn and drive toward the Kauffmans' farm, he followed the buggy. What Ruth was doing at her neighbor's farm was none of his business, but Leah's grandmother wasn't going where she told Leah she was.

*Maybe she had to stop in for a legitimate reason before visiting her friends*, his conscience warned him.

Maybe, but he didn't believe that. He slowed the truck when Ruth got out of her buggy and hurried toward the house. She went inside and didn't come back out.

James knew the smart thing to do was to keep going. Maybe he could convince Leah to listen to the complete story of his past.

He drove along the lane. If he had the chance to find out the truth about what Ruth was hiding, he could at least know that he'd helped Leah, though nothing could make up for the pain he'd inflicted on her.

As he neared the house, its front door opened and a lone person came out. It was Perry, James realized when he stopped the truck not far from Seth's hives.

The older man waited in the pool of light from the house until James had stepped out of the truck. "*Guten Owed.* I thought I recognized your truck. What can I do for you?"

James knew nothing but the truth would suffice. That was the hard lesson he'd learned from his and Leah's disastrous date.

"I saw Ruth's buggy coming here." He paused, then pushed the rest of the words out of his mouth. "It's Thursday evening."

Perry glanced toward the house as if trying to buy time before he had to answer. "So it is, and you're curious why Ruth came here when she told her granddaughter that she was going to be with her girlfriends."

"I am."

"Our ways are different from Englisch ones."

"I'm not sure what that has to do with Ruth not being honest with Leah."

"When you live in a community where gossip moves with unbelievable speed, when a couple is seeing each other, they try to do so in secret. It allows them to know if they're right for each other before everyone else has a chance to air their opinions on the match."

For a moment James was puzzled. Comprehension came like the first bit of starlight popping out of the darkness. "You're dating Ruth?"

"We don't speak of such things," said Leah's grandmother as she joined them. "Other than my friends, who have been willing to assist me, nobody else knows the truth."

"I understand," James said, trying to keep from smiling. Ruth's raised chin reminded him of Leah's when she was determined to do what she believed was right. "Perry was explaining it to me. Like I said, I understand, but your granddaughter doesn't. She's worried about you, Ruth."

The older couple looked at each other, and Perry arched a single snowy brow. Ruth's chin lowered from its defiant pose.

"You were right, Perry," she said.

He lifted that brow again.

Ruth gave him a wry grin. "I was wrong." She wagged a playful finger at Perry. "Me being wrong doesn't happen often, so there's no need to crow about it when it does."

"Am I crowing?" He looked at James.

James chuckled. "A wise man doesn't get involved in a lovers' spat that isn't his own."

Perry roared with laughter. Ruth rolled her eyes as if she were no older than Abby.

At the thought of his daughter, the image of her with Leah filled James's mind. He sobered as he looked at Ruth.

"Leah is worried about your safety," he said.

"And my sanity," the old woman replied in her usual no-nonsense tone. She gave him a wry smile. "It was silly to hope Leah wouldn't be curious. She was always that way as a Kind, eager to know everything about everything. That's why I got her interested in herbs. I knew the subject would intrigue her for a long time."

"Between you sneaking about," Perry said, "and how you've pushed me to persuade Seth to court Leah, she might be right about your sanity."

"Don't be silly." She put her hands on her hips and affixed James and Perry with a frown. "I'm not *ab im kopp*. I want Leah married before I get married for the second time."

So much instantly became clear to James. Leah had been puzzled about why her grandmother hadn't been honest in her letters, and once she arrived in Stony Brook, Leah had been confused about Ruth's matchmaking. Ruth had good intentions, but good intentions could lead to a terrible place.

"Whether or not Seth is the right man for her?" James knew he should keep his nose out of the Kauffman family's business, but he owed Leah a great debt for helping Abby smile again, even if they could never have a future together. He hadn't planned on repaying it this way. However, he couldn't turn away from his obligation.

"She's the last of my Kinskinder who remains unwed."

"But you, Perry..." He wasn't sure what to say, but he wanted to appeal to the man's common sense.

"I want Ruth to be happy." His simple words said more than a long explanation could have. "What do Englischers say? Happy wife, happy life?"

James nodded. How could he argue with Perry's kind heart that yearned to make the woman he loved happy? James hadn't gotten anywhere insisting that his own heart listen to reason.

"Will you tell Leah?" James asked.

Ruth shook her head. "No, I think *you* should tell her. Right away."

"Me? I thought—that is, I didn't think you approved of Leah spending time with me."

"I don't, but, as I told her last night, the decision has to be hers, and I trust her to make the right one."

Too startled to speak, James nodded again. He somehow got into his truck without tripping over his feet, which suddenly seemed as awkward as a toddler's. Starting his truck, he turned it around to drive away. He looked at the yard, but Perry and Ruth had gone inside for their date.

Nothing remained but for him to go next door and ease Leah's worries about her grandmother. He hoped it wouldn't be their final conversation, but if it was, he wouldn't hide how he felt about her. There had been enough secrets. It was time for the truth.

---

Leah held Abby's hand as they walked out the door. She carried a flashlight, because they were going to the phone shack out near the road, and she didn't want to chance the driver of a passing vehicle not seeing them.

James was late.

He was never late.

Maybe he'd left a message on the answering machine Ruth shared with the Eichers.

In the distance, a car engine rumbled in the darkness. What if James had had trouble with his truck?

Abby tugged on her sleeve and pointed.

Leah breathed a prayer of gratitude as the flash of lights turning into the farm lane announced that James had arrived to collect his daughter.

Relief flooded Leah, and her shoulders ached as they sagged. She hadn't realized how taut they'd become as she'd struggled not to keep looking at the clock in the kitchen. She hadn't wanted to upset Abby when there could have been many reasons why her father was delayed.

Leading the little girl toward the house, they reached the front yard just as James did. Instead of speaking to Leah, he said, "Go in the house, Abby, and put your things in your backpack."

Abby looked at Leah, consternation on her face.

Comprehending what Abby wasn't going to say, Leah nodded.

"You can take home the cookies we made for you and your Daed." Her gaze shifted to James. "We made the almond puffs you like so much."

Abby almost danced into the house with her excitement.

"You're late," Leah said as soon as she heard the door close behind Abby. "I was starting to get worried."

"I got distracted on my way home."

"By what?"

"Your grandmother."

She looked at him in astonishment. Her amazement grew while she listened to James explain how he'd happened to see the Kauffmans' buggy going to the Eichers' farm. All along Ruth had been going no farther away than the Eicher farm on Thursday evenings, taking a long, roundabout route to a back road so nobody would guess she was actually heading next door. When James related what Ruth and Perry had told him about their courtship and their plans for their grandchildren, she backed toward the porch steps. She grabbed the rail, then slowly sank down to sit on the steps.

James crossed the yard and leaned his arm on the newel post. "I know you're shocked, Leah."

"Shocked is an understatement."

"Don't be angry—"

Laughter exploded out of her. Tears squeezed from the corners of her eyes, and she couldn't stop laughing at the silliness of the past few weeks.

He stared at her in disbelief. Had she lost her mind?

"I'm not angry," she finally said. "Seth and I knew our grandparents were conspiring to make a match for us, but we had no idea why they were so set on it."

"You said you were shocked."

"I knew Grossmammi was lonely, and I wanted her to find someone.

I never guessed she needed to see me wed before she would marry Perry."

"She wants you to be happy." He sat beside her, leaving enough room between them so their shoulders didn't touch.

Leah longed for him to put his arms around her and hold her against him until her doubts and questions vanished, but that would be impossible. His past had opened a chasm between them.

"I know," she replied, but she wondered if she could be happy without James in her life.

Yet how could she be in love with a man who had set aside his beliefs?

As if she'd asked aloud, James said, "I know you were upset last night when I mentioned the army. Will you let me tell you everything about that time? Will you listen?"

Shame coursed through her, hot and scathing. She'd acted badly at the restaurant, storming out without giving him a chance to explain.

"Tell me everything," she whispered.

# 16

After hours of waiting for his opportunity to be honest with Leah, James faltered before he could speak a single word. He'd practiced over and over in his head while driving to and from Miami University what he would say to her and how he would choose the best words to let her know he empathized with her dismay. To reassure her that her worst fears weren't true. Other parts of his faith had suffered since before Connie's death, but not his Mennonite pacifism.

Now as they sat face to face, he knew only the unvarnished truth would suffice. If he tried to whitewash what had happened and why, he could lose his last chance to heal the pain he'd caused.

He gazed a moment longer into her eyes, eyes that evoked so many emotions within him as they displayed the ones inside her. He hadn't expected her to laugh when he told her about what was behind Ruth's Thursday evenings and the scheme for Leah and Seth to marry. In fact, he hadn't dared to hope he'd hear her sweet laugh again. Not after their disastrous evening. He wanted to apologize for that and many other things, but easing his conscience would have to wait.

"Leah—"

"Let me say something first." She put slender fingers on his arm, and warmth spread into the icy void surrounding his heart. "James, I'm sorry."

"You? You're sorry? Why?"

"I shouldn't have scurried away like a frightened rabbit. I knew you had more to tell me. I should have stayed and listened. Really listened." She looked at him. "I'd like to hear your story, James. All of it."

Rubbing his dry eyes, he thought of the many tears he'd shed during the years he was about to share with her.

Every instinct told James to keep staring across the yard so he wouldn't chance seeing her revulsion again. But he wouldn't hide from her anymore. He gazed into her expressive eyes, seeing his uncertainty mirrored in them.

"I had a wonderful childhood," he said, "and I assumed my whole life would be blessed. I enjoyed school and received a full scholarship to a college here in Indiana. I was extra excited because that meant I could attend with my best friend."

A lump of emotion clogged his throat, preventing him from continuing. He tried to swallow it, but the lump didn't want to move.

"Did you and your friend have a *gut* time at college?"

Somehow, her question freed him to answer in a choked voice he knew could give out at any moment. "We did. I met Connie in college, and he met the girl he planned to marry."

"He didn't marry her?"

"He didn't have the chance."

Pain flickered in Leah's eyes as she whispered, "Why?"

"My friend's name was Brian Zebulske." He cleared his throat before adding, "Sergeant Brian Zebulske."

"A soldier?"

"A brave soldier. Before he left for the Middle East, he asked me to forgive him for choosing that life. He knew that, as a Mennonite, I'd never fight by his side."

"You said *you* were in the army. James, I'm confused."

Admitting that he was confused too would only delay what he must tell her. He wasn't confounded about his past, however. He was bewildered about his future and whether there was any chance of this beautiful woman being a part of it.

"*With* the army. I worked *with* the army," he said, knowing he had to concentrate on the topic at hand. There would be time—he hoped—for discussing the future once he said what he'd come to tell her. "I'll explain the difference in a moment." Again he had to struggle to speak around the weight filling his throat. "The day before Brian left for his deployment overseas, I told him that he was my best friend, and though I couldn't support his choice, I'd pray for him."

"I'm sure you prayed every day that he'd come home safe."

"I did, but God had other plans for Brian. When I heard of his death, I knew I couldn't let his sacrifice be in vain." He stared into her eyes, desperate for her to understand his loss so she'd realize why he'd done what he'd done. "Brian died trying to rescue his men when their vehicle struck an IED. An improvised explosive device."

Leah shivered as if the temperature had dropped twenty degrees. "I know what an IED is. I've read about them in the newspaper."

To keep himself from putting his arms around her in an attempt to banish the ice that surrounded them as he spoke of the first horrible loss he'd suffered, he clasped his hands on his left knee. "I asked God to help me find a way to honor Brian's memory, though my faith took a big hit when I heard about his death."

"You were angry with God?"

He nodded and sighed. "I know what God sees is far beyond what we can, and He mourns the loss of a single creature, but I'd prayed so hard for Brian to come home safe again. I hadn't wanted him to go in the first place."

"If he hadn't been there, those men could have died."

"I know, and that confused me more. Brian did save those men's lives, but I lost my best friend."

"And your faith?"

"Not completely. That happened later."

"When you were in—with the army?"

He shook his head. "My time working with the army consisted of two jobs. One as an orderly in a rehab hospital where wounded soldiers came to learn to walk and talk and take care of themselves again. The other, the one I truly enjoyed and led to my plans to fix up my house in Stony Brook, was when I volunteered with a group rebuilding homes to meet the special needs for the men and women I met during their rehabilitation. I never wore a uniform other than a lab coat or a tool belt. It was a way to honor my friend's memory and try to continue his work of saving lives."

"Without actually taking up arms yourself."

"Yes, and I'm glad I had the opportunity to help save lives, even though it delayed me getting my master's degree and now my PhD. I'd married Connie before Brian was killed. She helped me hold onto the tatters of my faith and stood by me when I took a break in my studies to honor his memory, but she got sick shortly after Abby turned three. I was back at school by then. I wanted to take more time off, but Connie insisted that I keep going." His voice cracked. "Then she died. I couldn't see why she had to suffer and die, and my faith failed me. Can you understand, Leah?"

---

Leah knew words would be futile, so she put her hand over the top of his clenched ones. His fingers relaxed beneath hers. He slid his right hand out and put it over hers.

"I understand," she whispered. "I was angry too, when Mamm died.

I was Abby's age. It took me a long time to know that not forgiving God was making me unhappy. Then I realized there was nothing to forgive. His ways aren't something we can comprehend, but we can be sure of one thing. His ways are filled with love and grace."

"You believe that?"

"With all my heart." She raised one hand and cupped his cheek. "I'm so sorry, James, for the way I've acted. I know that was difficult to talk about, and I'm grateful you did."

"I wasn't sure if I'd ever be able to speak of how my faith was knocked for a loop when Brian died."

"You must have told Connie."

"I planned to, but she got sick. I couldn't burden her with my grief when she was dealing with tumors, surgery, and chemotherapy."

"She had cancer?"

"Yes." He stood, but she remained where she was, knowing he needed to work out his tension by pacing. As much as she wanted to help, there wasn't anything she could do now other than let him keep talking. "No matter what anyone says, I know she didn't plan to kill herself. I told the cops and anyone else who asked that she was trying to keep from dying. The first rounds of chemo made her sicker, and the radiation stole every bit of her energy, but she was determined to live each day she'd been granted."

"The accident—"

"It must have been an accident, though nobody else seemed to believe it. Even if she was desperate enough to want to end her own life, she would never endanger Abby. Maybe her car went off the shoulder and she lost control. Somehow Abby escaped. When she stopped talking everyone was confounded, though one doctor labeled it post-traumatic stress." He laughed without humor. "When I tried to argue, I was treated as if I was too blinded by loyalty to Connie to see the obvious truth. I *was* loyal to Connie, and that's why I kept asking the questions."

"One person knows the truth."

"I know, but even if Abby did talk about what happened, she's a little girl, and she may not be able to tell us anything."

Tears burned in Leah's eyes. "So many were hurt by that accident."

He knelt in front of her and framed her face with his broad hands. "Leah, I want you to know I never intended to hurt you. I would do anything *not* to hurt you. I love you."

Her breath caught as she gazed at him. In the light coming through the living room windows, she could see the truth on his face. He did love her.

"I—"

He put a finger to her lips. "Don't say it, Leah. I know your life is with the Amish, and I'm an Englischer. I know we can't be together. I've made a mess of your life, so maybe I should accept the job offer I've been given. Abby and I can move away and get out of your life for good."

"No!"

The childish cry came from the porch, and Leah looked over her shoulder as James jumped to his feet.

Abby had spoken!

Rising, Leah pressed her fingers to her lips as James reached his daughter in a single leap up the steps.

"Abby, say something else," he urged.

Looking past her dad, the little girl gulped loudly. In a voice hoarse from disuse, she said, "I want to stay. You too, Daddy, and Leah." She sank to the porch. "Oh no, Mommy! I'm sorry."

James sat and picked up his daughter. He held her with her head against his heart. "You've nothing to be sorry for, Abby. Your mommy loved you."

"No," the child argued.

"It's true, Abby. She loved you. You did nothing wrong."

"Not true."

When James started to protest again, Leah grasped his shoulder. He stopped.

"Abby," Leah said, "you know your Mamm loved you, ain't so?"

The little girl nodded.

"You believe you did something wrong?"

Abby nodded again.

"Something connected with the car accident? Tell us about it, Liebling."

Hoping she hadn't pushed too hard, Leah held her breath. It eased out when Abby began to talk, but sadness welled up inside her as she listened to the little girl.

"We went to get special food for you, Daddy." She raised the bag of cookies she'd brought from the house. "Mommy liked to make you special treats like Leah does."

"What happened before the car hit the fence?" he asked.

"Didn't hit the fence. White car hit us."

Over Abby's head, James exchanged an astonished glance with Leah. She heard him gulp before he asked, "A white car?"

"White and big. Mommy screamed. Told me to hold on. We hit the tree."

"Then you climbed out of the car?"

Abby shook her head. "No, the man helped me out."

"Man?" Leah asked at the same time James did.

"Man with the white car. He came over and checked the car. He looked at Mommy, and he looked at me. He helped me out. He smelled funny, Daddy."

"Funny how?" Leah kept her voice soft, not wanting to overwhelm the little girl.

"Funny bad." Abby shrugged. "He asked if I was okay, and I said yes." Her gaze fell to the floor. "He said not to tell anyone about him or Mommy wouldn't go to heaven. Now I told. Mommy won't be an angel." She began to cry.

Leah's stomach rebelled at the idea of someone saying something so horrible to a Kind who'd seen her Mamm die.

Beside her, James groaned and held Abby closer. He pressed his head against her hair, rocking her as she wept.

Praying for God to give her the right words, Leah leaned in and brushed Abby's hair from her wet face. The little girl looked at her with haunted eyes. The poor, dear Kind had been keeping this secret for over a year, unable to share it with anyone for fear of what would happen to her mother.

"God loves you, Abby," she said. "He loves you more than you can imagine. He wouldn't do anything to hurt you or your Mamm or your Daed. When we hurt, God hurts too, because He wants us to be filled with the joy of knowing Him and knowing He'll always be with us. Your Mamm is with God in heaven, and she knows the joy of being showered by His grace. You telling us the truth doesn't change that." Wiping away the little girl's tears, she whispered, "She's watching you, and she's happy you're letting joy back inside you."

Abby gave a sudden giggle when Leah tapped her chest. "Mommy happy?"

"Ja, and she wants you and your Daed to be happy too."

The little girl threw her arms around Leah, hugging her so hard that Leah found it impossible to breathe. Looking past Abby, Leah saw James smile. It was the most wonderful sight she'd ever seen.

"Abby?" James asked in a cautious tone. "Do you remember what the man looked like?"

Abby stiffened, and Leah bent to place a kiss on her hair and whisper it was okay—she was safe.

"Big like his big, white car. And he smelled bad."

"Did you look at his face?"

She nodded.

"What color were his eyes?"

"Blue." Her forehead furrowed. "He had a hole beneath this one." She touched the skin beneath her left eye.

Leah drew in a jagged breath but said nothing as James guided his daughter to build upon her description of the man who'd driven Connie off the road. When Abby mentioned he had a shortened finger on his left hand, Leah hurt inside.

Standing, James drew Leah to her feet. "Your face tells me that you agree: Her description matches Willard Eicher."

"It does, but will anyone believe her?"

"I do. You do. That's enough for now." He hooked a thumb toward his truck. "Keep Abby here. I'm going to the Eichers' farm."

She grabbed his sleeve. "Not tonight, James. Grossmammi is there. I don't want her to be caught in the middle of this."

"But—"

"And if Willard sees you and suspects why you're there, he can slip away in the darkness. Let's go tomorrow when we can look for proof."

"I don't want to wait any longer."

"Trust me on this, James. Nobody knows what Abby has told us, and we'll be better poking around in the daylight, when we can say we're studying plants."

"Poking around for what?"

"The white car. Seth told me his brother sold his car, but if Willard caused the accident and hit Connie's car hard enough to send it off the road, there must be telling damage on his car too. He couldn't sell it without arousing suspicion."

"You think he still has it?"

"Ja, and I think I know where it is."

# 17

Everything was arranged—more easily than James had expected. Dorcas agreed to watch Abby for the afternoon. The little girl said nothing when James left her at the bed-and-breakfast. Though he hadn't asked his daughter to pretend she was mute, Abby seemed to understand it would be better if nobody but he and Leah knew she was talking again.

Leah was waiting by the round barn when he pulled to a stop by the house. The air was filled with a chilly mist, but it wasn't as icy as the anticipation within him. They needed to find the proof of the crime. His suggestion that they contact the authorities had been vetoed by Leah, who warned him that the Amish didn't seek help from the police unless absolutely necessary.

"Besides," she added, "if Willard sees a police car coming to the farm, he'll bolt."

"They'll catch him."

"If they believe us."

He couldn't argue with that. Accusing a man who came from a respected plain family was difficult enough, but it became more complicated when his accuser was a young child who hadn't spoken in a year.

So they'd do it Leah's way first. She'd asked him to trust her, and he'd try.

Slipping along the line of trees edging the field, James held his flashlight and double-checked that his cell phone was in his pocket. He intended to make use of its camera. He was grateful when it began to rain in earnest as they crossed from one farm to the other. The storm would keep the Eichers inside, and it was unlikely they'd look out the window when all there was to see was rain. The bees would be in their hives, and Seth wouldn't have any reason to check on them.

They paused at the edge of the trees. In front of them was the rickety barn where Seth had put the swarm while he acclimated them to their new home.

"There," Leah said.

"That barn? One half of it is empty, and Seth said the other side was full of old farm equipment."

"Seth actually said he'd *guess* his Grossdawdi stored old equipment in there. He also said he hadn't been in there in ages." She wrapped her arms around herself and shook her head so raindrops didn't fall from her kerchief onto her nose. "I don't like sneaking about."

"I don't either, but God has led us here. Would He want us to turn around and leave?"

"You believe God is with us?" Leah asked, startled.

"How can I question if God cares about me when He has brought you into our lives?" He tilted her face and gave her a swift kiss that promised it wouldn't be the last one they shared.

"He knows the state of our hearts," she said in not much more than a whisper. "My heart may not have the courage to do this a second time."

He laughed. "You're the most fearless person I know. When you believe something is right, you don't hesitate."

Without another word, he seized her hand and led her across the yard at a run, ducking behind the hives in case one of the Eichers might look out toward them. They reached the far side of the barn and pressed against the unpainted boards. Rain poured on them from the roof's overhang.

He inched toward a door and grasped the latch. It wouldn't move. Was it locked or rusted shut? No matter. He put his shoulder against the door and shoved. With a crack, the board beneath his shoulder gave way, vanishing into the darkness on the other side of the door. He stepped back so he could snake his arm through the hole and grope for the latch.

The click of it unlocking seemed as loud as thunder. With a glance at Leah, who nodded, he lifted the latch and drew the door open.

A cloud of dust exploded, and he wondered how long it'd been since anyone had gone in. He switched on his flashlight and stepped inside.

It wasn't completely dark. The boards along the side of the barn were warped enough to let stripes of gray light into the large space. When he caught sight of the glint of metal, he focused his flashlight on it.

"A car!" Leah said from behind him.

It was a gargantuan white Cadillac that had to be at least fifty years old. Made of solid steel, it would be a weapon in the hands of a careless driver.

James paused. The white paint on Connie's car had been on the driver's side.

"I didn't ask Abby if the other car was coming toward them or beside them," he grumbled. "You check the passenger's side, and I'll check the driver's side." He handed the flashlight to Leah and switched on his phone's light.

"There's a big scratch over here," Leah said.

He was about to reply when he saw blue paint on the fender in front of him. He activated his camera and snapped a few photos. "That's the same color as Connie's car."

"Why would the paint be scraped off over here?" She straightened and looked over the wide hood to him. "You said the police believed Connie hit a fence and then went off the road, right?"

"I saw the fence. The paint was off in a couple of places."

"Willard hit Connie's car, and then to make it look as if no other car was involved, he ran his car against the fence so it looked like she had run into it."

Before James could reply, a furious roar came from the door. A dark figure jumped toward Leah, raising a hand.

"No!" shouted James, but the figure didn't slow down as he continued his attack on her.

Leah whirled to see Willard barreling toward her like a maddened bull. His face was distorted with rage and fear. Terrified, she shone her flashlight in his eyes and took a quick step to the side. Blinded, he hit the car and fell to the floor.

He jumped up before she could move and shoved her as he sprinted back toward the door. She was knocked off her feet and hit the floor hard as Willard stampeded out of the barn.

"Are you all right?" James asked.

They couldn't let Willard get away. "I'm fine. Go!"

James raced past her. Leah pushed herself to her feet, wincing as her right hip protested. She tried to ignore it and ran after the two men.

Bursting out of the barn, she skidded to a stop on the wet grass and gaped at an astounding sight. Perry and James were holding Willard's arms behind him as Seth smoked the bees in one of his hives. In his panic, Willard must have run right into it. Welts were visible on his face and hands where bees had stung him.

"It's safe," Seth said, motioning for her to join them. "The bees are calming nicely."

"What's going on?" Perry looked from her to James and then to Willard. "Why are you out running around in the rain?"

It didn't take long to explain. Seth was sent to call the police and to pick up Abby from Dorcus and bring her to Ruth's house. Willard cursed his Grossdawdi and his brother as well as James and Leah. None of them responded.

The police arrived quickly. They listened to James's account, checked the barn, and arrested Willard, putting him in the back of one of their patrol cars. Leah saw the policemen's surprise when Perry asked to go with them so his raving grandson—who was calling his Grossdawdi horrible names—wouldn't be alone at the police station. Perry left in a different car while two officers went with Seth to examine the car in the barn after asking Leah and James to wait for them at the Kauffmans' house.

James put his arm around Leah's shoulders, keeping her close as they crossed the open field. "Are you okay?" he asked.

"I'm going to be a bit stiff tomorrow after hitting the floor, but I'll be fine."

"You're hurt!"

"Just bumped."

"I couldn't have guessed that by how fast you ran after us."

She looked at him. "I wanted to make sure *you* weren't hurt."

"Did you think I'd strike him?"

She shook her head as she put her hands on his arms. "I know you're a man of peace, James. When your best friend was killed, you channeled your grief into finding a way to heal others instead of hurting them. You're a brilliant man with a great heart."

"You think I'm brilliant?"

She smiled. "Ja."

"Then listen to my brilliant advice when I say it's time to get you home. Your grandmother is on the fence about me as it is, and if I keep you out in the rain until you catch a cold, she'll never forgive me."

With a laugh, she walked with him across the field. He didn't look back at the barn that housed the car involved with his wife's death, and neither did Leah.

***

"You need more Kaffi, James," Ruth murmured, clucking over him like a hen with a single chick. "It'll warm you after getting soaked."

Leah winked at him. His words about Ruth had been wrong. As soon as he and Leah had come into the kitchen and told the story of their search yet again, the older woman had insisted on Leah taking a warm shower before she got sick. Leah had, and then Ruth ordered James to do the same. He was finished by the time the police and Seth, who brought Abby, arrived.

Now two officers sat at the kitchen table as if they were regular visitors. Both had steaming cups of coffee in front of them along with large servings of a blueberry pie Ruth had prepared while the others were questioned. The policemen were gentle with Abby, who sat on James's lap while they led her through the events of the accident again. Her tears became a grin when they gave her a plastic badge that was a miniature of the ones the officers wore.

Rising, Leah poured another partial cup of cocoa for Abby. The child's "thank you" was so soft Leah wasn't sure she'd heard it until she saw James smile.

Neither of them could know how long it would take for Abby to speak as a child her age should. The trauma of witnessing her mother's death and then seeing the man responsible for it would require those around her to have understanding and patience while she continued to heal from wounds they couldn't see.

Abby was blessed with a father who had both compassion and plenty of patience.

Sitting beside Ruth, Leah listened while the officers spoke to Seth. "I had no idea the car was there," Seth said. "Please believe me."

"We do," Leah replied, then looked at her folded hands when one of the policemen shot a frown in her direction.

Seth gave her the hint of a smile. "I'm glad to hear that." Looking at James, he added, "My brother believed that nobody would risk going past the bees, so the car wouldn't be found in the barn."

The older policeman turned a page in his notebook. "One thing I don't quite get. If Abby was here at the farm often and she went to the Eichers' farm, why didn't she see Willard?"

"I don't know," Leah said, and James shook his head.

"I know." Seth took a deep breath and squared his shoulders. "My brother kept asking me if I knew when Leah would be watching Abby. I thought it was because he wanted to spend time with Leah, but I realize now he had another reason for asking." He sighed. "So many lies and so much unhappiness, and none of it would have happened if my brother hadn't been out all night drinking with his Englisch friends before he drove that day."

"He was drunk?" James asked before turning to Leah. "That must be why Abby said he smelled funny."

Even though everyone was watching, Leah took his hand and gave it a gentle squeeze. When he brushed a single fingertip against her cheek, she was startled to see it was wet with her tears. He handed her a handkerchief, and she whispered her thanks.

Across the table, Seth said as if to himself, "Willard obviously banged into the fence with his car to make it look as if Mrs. Holden hit the fence and lost control. He thought he'd cover his tracks and avoid going to prison. All he did was make everything worse." He looked up and said, "James, I'm so sorry."

James nodded, accepting the apology. Fortunately, there weren't many more questions. Once the policemen had finished their pie and had accepted another serving in a box from Ruth, they left. Seth stood too, saying he wanted to check on his bees.

Before he left, Leah took him aside and shared with him her conversation with Dorcas. Seth wore an infatuated grin when Leah told him how Dorcas loved him. Leah was sure her friend and her neighbor would soon find an excuse to ride home from a singing together.

Grossmammi Ruth pushed herself to her feet. "If you'll excuse me, I need to spend some time in prayer for Perry and his grandsons." She squeezed Leah's shoulder as she walked past her and up the stairs.

Abby got off James's lap and went into the front room where she selected one of the schoolbooks and opened it. She began quietly reading aloud to herself.

Smiling, James stood and came around the table to sit beside Leah. "I don't think I'll ever get tired of her voice. Okay, maybe I will by the time she's a whiny teenager, so I'd appreciate it if you didn't remind me I said that today."

"I'll try to remember." She blinked back tears of joy at the thought of spending time with the Holdens in the years to come. "How are you doing?"

"Happy and sad at the same time. Happy to know the truth, but sad it doesn't change anything that happened."

She whispered, "I'm sorry. I know how much you loved Connie."

"I love her still. I don't think I'll ever stop loving her."

Leah made sure none of her heated tears fell. Was that James's way of telling her that, although he'd told Leah he loved her, it wasn't in the same way he'd loved Connie?

"While we've got a chance to talk alone," he went on, "there's something I haven't told you about, Leah."

"More?" As soon as the word left her mouth, she looked stricken. "James, I'm sorry. I didn't mean it that way."

"No, you have every right to ask." He gave her a rueful smile. "I told you a little about this when we were at the restaurant, but not everything because the second letter didn't arrive until this morning's mail. It helped me make up my mind about the earlier one." He pulled two envelopes from his pocket. "Read the top one first."

She did, and her heart lurched when she read the job offer from the renowned college in Kansas. It was everything James had been working toward for years—a full professorship teaching the courses that allowed him to pass along his knowledge to his students.

"Congratulations, James. Have you decided if you're going to take the job?"

"Before I answer, read what I got this morning."

She took the other envelope and opened the second sheet. Her eyes widened when she realized the letter was an acceptance for Abby to attend the college's elementary school. The letter outlined ways the teachers and staff could help the little girl learn in spite of her not talking.

"So much thought has gone into their plan for Abby," she said. "You're going to accept, aren't you?" She folded the second letter.

"I will, assuming they'll arrange for a third offer."

"For what?" She touched the envelopes, then pulled back her fingers when she saw how they trembled. "It seems as if you've gotten all you hoped for, James."

"All I *prayed* for." He smiled. "Or almost all."

"Prayed?"

He nodded. "My faith may be as small as the proverbial mustard seed, but I'm trying to nurture it, knowing God is with me."

"You've got a job, Abby's school, your faith—what more do you want?"

He went to Abby's backpack and pulled out a paperback book. Bringing it to the table, he flipped it to a page marked with a sticky note. He turned the book so she could read the words at the top of the page.

She gasped when she realized it was a course catalog from the college that had offered James a teaching position. The program listed on the marked page was for a bachelor's degree in health and nutrition. Several classes had been highlighted, classes about using herbs. Grasping the book, she pulled it toward her as she devoured every word.

"I can help you study for your GED," he said. "You'll need that, but with your experience, you'll be able to skip some intro courses and get your degree more quickly. If it's what you want."

It was what she wanted, but was it what God wanted for her?

Grossmammi's words whispered to her from her memory: *Have faith the answer will become clear, and you'll know within your heart what God expects of you. One thing I've learned in the years I've lived is never to doubt that an answer will come. I need to believe it will and that I can accept the answer when it does.*

Leah's heart pounded. Had the advice been Grossmammi's way of saying she would support whatever choice Leah made to follow the will of God? She dared to believe so.

"I know it means a great sacrifice for you to do this," James said. "From what you've said, I know you changed your plans to come here."

"I'd intended to join my friends in baptismal classes. If I'd been baptized, going to college would mean risking being put under the Bann. But because I haven't been baptized, I won't be ostracized."

"What about your family?" His gaze searched her face as if trying to discover the answer before she spoke.

"Daed and my siblings might not be thrilled with me going to college, but they love me and want what is best for me. Grossmammi has urged me to follow the path God has for me. I think that path leads me to continuing to learn about herbs so I can help others." She smiled. "Just as He led you on a path to help others, James."

"Does that mean you want to apply?"

She didn't hesitate. "It does. I've learned that God brings us to the place we should be and into the lives of those He knows we can help."

"And who can help us."

She smiled. "As you've helped me, James. I want to live a plain life. Loving God and serving Him are things I plan to continue doing the rest of my life, but He put this yearning to learn more about herbs into my heart."

"Will you consider living the rest of your life with me and Abby?" He knelt before her. "We won't ever be Amish as you've been, but we'll find a Mennonite church where we all can be comfortable. You can teach us to live a plainer life. Would you like that?"

"I would love it, James." Bending forward, she framed his face with her hands. "Just as I love you."

He gazed at her, the answer to her dreams in his adoring eyes. "I don't have a ring, my love, because I know it's not your way, but will you marry me? I love you, and I'll love you forever."

"As you'll love Connie forever?"

"Yes. Does that bother you?"

"No! You wouldn't be the man I love, James Holden, if you didn't love her forever. I'll be glad to share your heart with Connie and with Abby."

"And any others who come into our lives?"

"As many little ones as God blesses us with. I love you, and I want to be your wife and the Mamm to your Kinder."

Standing, he brought her to her feet and into his arms. When his lips found hers, she knew she'd found everything she'd sought. She hadn't guessed a man with a broken heart and his sweet, silent daughter would quietly heal hers and open it to a love she'd treasure for the rest of her life.